The Red Murders
John Robichaud Mysteries

H. Paul Doucette

BWL Publishing Inc.

Books we love to writ...
Authors around the ....

http://bwlpublishing.ca

Amazon print 9780228626626
BWL Print 9780228626633
Ingram Spark 9780228626640
Barnes & Noble 9780228626657

Copyright 2023 H. Paul Doucette
Cover art by Pandora Designs

Disclaimer

This is a work of fiction and a product of the Author's imagination. Names of places, events and locations used in this story are factual and have been taken from historical records. The names of people and certain positions are fictitious and any resemblance to persons living or dead is unintentional and entirely coincidental.

Dedication

To those who fought in the shadows; they also served

Table of Contents

"Where do we find allies?"
Father Yarvi smiled. "Among our
enemies, where else?"

Prologue

November 1944, Arkhangelsk, Russia
The room was not much more than a deep hole in the earth: a root cellar under an old wooden farm house in a small fishing village ten miles outside the city. The only access was by a trap door in the floor above with a ladder nailed to the joist. At the moment, it was dimly lit by two oil lanterns above a table, the only piece of furniture in the cellar. The lanterns hung from one of three broad oak beams that supported the floor above. The table was surrounded by a half dozen wooden casks and crates and a couple of crude wicker baskets piled on the earthen floor. A large wicker wrapped bottle of home brewed vodka sat on top of it.

The air in the cellar was cold, still. The fumes from the lanterns mingled with the acrid smoke from the harsh Turkish tobacco cigarettes a few of the occupants were smoking, adding to the stale smells of seawater, ropes, and other fishing gear.

"They have to get away from here," one of the men said in a loud angry voice, slapping his hand on the table for emphasis. "The information must get out."

Four men sat around the table on whatever they could grab while two young men stood to the side behind an old man. All were dressed in shubas, ushankas, coats and hats that most of the local peasantry wore, and thick black leather boots or verenkls. The men were engaged in a heated discussion about the fate of the two young men standing behind them.

The two young men were brothers; Gregori and Ivan Greshenko from a farming district southeast of Arkhangelsk. Two weeks ago, they witnessed a raid by the Red Guard that happened in the small village of Sya where their parents lived. The Guard swooped into town demanding that all wheat stored there be surrendered to them. When some farmers refused the Guard set about killing them and everyone else they could find, then loaded the wheat and left. That's when Gregori, the eldest, took his brother and fled to a nearby village where one of the residents helped them flee to a fishing village called, Lichka, where his brother lived and who owned a boat.

When they arrived and told their story of what the communists were doing, a meeting of the village elders was called to decide what to do with them and their information. They all agreed that, if at all possible, this information must be given to the outside world.

"Yes," another man said. He was the oldest man there, judging by the full white beard he wore. His name was Dmitri Volkov, the village starost, or elder. "We agree. The information they have must get out. The question is how?"

"The border is out of the question," another said. "I have been told the NKVD have increased their watch and patrols there."

The room went quiet for a few moments, then one man leaned in. "It may be possible to stow them away on one of the ships due to sail back to the United States."

"Impossible Igor," said another. His name was Josef Golubev. "The docks are controlled by the communists. They would be taken before they could reach a ship."

"Maybe not," Igor said. "I think there might be away to get them on board unseen."

"Explain," said the old man.

"There is a ship in port arrived with the last convoy. It is the fourth time it has made the voyage. I know the captain. He is an American who is opposed to the communists. He has helped in the past; mostly taking letters to families who fled to America. I can approach him and ask his help."

"And you say this man can be trusted?" Volkov asked.

"*Da.*"

"Even if this be true," Josef said, "how do we get them to the ship? The Red Guard watches everything on the docks and there are so many informers."

"True," Igor said. "The only way I can think of is by boat. We get one of our people to take them by boat into the harbour then alongside the ship where they board. Once on board they will be safe."

"It could be dangerous," the fourth man said.

"Yes, but any plan will be dangerous. This seems the least risky option," Volkov said. "It is settled then. Igor, you will make contact with this captain?"

"*Da.*"

Josef, you see to arranging for the boat. Now. When?"

"The ship is still off-loading its cargo," Igor said. "According to the harbour master, the return convoy is due to sail in four days. I think it best if we deliver these men on the last night at least two hours before they let go."

The old man turned on his seat and looked behind him at the two young men standing there.

"This means staying with us a bit longer, da?" he said.

They both nodded.

The plan was put into effect.

In another room in a drab three story building in Moscow, a man stood at attention in front of a large wooden desk; his eyes fixed on an indefinite point on the wall behind the uniformed officer sitting at the desk.

"Comrade Petrov," the officer said without looking up. "You have an impressive record of service to the party."

"*Spasibo*, Comrade Colonel," Petrov said.

"I see here you speak English," the Colonel stated in English. "Where did you learn."

"My parents were part of a diplomatic delegation in Poland. I was sent to the English school there," Petrov answered in English.

"Good. You have been selected for a mission which will take you to Canada. You are to go to the port city of Halifax in Nova Scotia. This is the allies main convoy port and British Naval Base. Once there you will obtain as much information on the new technologies their navy is developing. You will send whatever you obtain back through our diplomatic mission in Ottawa."

"Yes sir."

"Yes sir." He did not ask why. He did not need to know; it was enough that the party deemed their deaths were necessary.

"You will go to Murmansk immediately where you will sign on one of our merchant ships that is readying its return crossing to

11

Canada, then upon arrival, make your way to Halifax."

"Yes sir."

The colonel opened a drawer and took out a large envelope and passed it to him.

"Your papers are inside as well as your contact information and some Canadian currency. Good luck."

"Thank you, Comrade Colonel." He clicked his heels and gave him a sharp salute then did an about turn and marched smartly from the office.

Petrov arrived in Montreal in early September and jumped ship with the help of the ship's captain, who was also an agent with the NKVD. He put him in touch with a Soviet cell set up in the port. These people helped him put together a plan for getting him to Halifax. During his time in Montreal, he met a French woman, Celeste Dumont. She was a member of a radical leftist group whose goal was the independence of Quebec from Canada. They very quickly became lovers.

When the day came for him to depart, she said she wanted to leave with him. He agreed.

Chapter One

November 1944, Halifax, Nova Scotia

It was a cold black night. Above, the starkly white stars glinted in the cloudless sky. The man standing just inside the recessed doorway wore a heavy woolen overcoat and cap with its flaps pulled low over his ears. He hugged himself as he stomped his feet, happy they were inside thick lined boots. Clouds of vapour almost crackled in the frigid air as he slowly exhaled.

Larry Mitchell was thirty-six years old, single, a little on the heavy side but otherwise in good condition. He had a good job, working between the shipyards and HMC Dockyard as an electrician with some training as an electronics technician. That meant he made good money and exempted him from military service which, truth be told, he did not mind at all.

"Damn it," he muttered out loud, checking his wristwatch for the third time; it read 4:20. "Where the hell is he?"

He did not like the cold nor did he like standing around; skulking in the shadows, hoping no passing policemen noticed him. His senses were alert to any sound, any movement, leaving him feeling tense, edgy. He was not a patient man even at the best of times and now he felt less so because he was tired and cold.

Not for the first time tonight, he found himself thinking of the sexy young woman sleeping in his bed.

He met her a couple of weeks ago at the Green Lantern lunch counter on Barrington Street where she worked as a waitress. Her name was Celeste Dumont. He struck up a conversation with her in French which thrilled her. Lucky for him, he thought, he had worked in Laval at the shipyards as an electrician for ten years and picked enough of the language to live there.

She agreed to see him outside of work and not long after they became lovers. He could not believe his luck since he never thought of himself as the type of man to attractive a young beauty. If she had any flaw, it was her expensive appetites. That was a month ago.

A week later she introduced him to the Russian. Nikolai Petrov.

Petrov was a big burly man in his mid-forties with strong Slavic facial features. He appeared friendly enough at their first meeting but it was not long before Mitchell sensed there was something sinister, dangerous about him.

At first, he was friendly enough, claiming to be a merchant seaman who missed his ship and was 'beached' for now. The three of them started to hang out together, drinking, dancing and generally enjoying themselves. Later, the Russian would leave, and Larry and Celeste would head for her room for more wild sex.

It was on the third night they were at the speakeasy, sitting in a darkened corner when Petrov made his true purpose known. He asked him if Larry was interested in making some money on the side.

"Hell yeah," Mitchell said. He had already drunk four glasses of beer and a shot of Vodka that Petrov had tucked inside his coat. "What do I hafta do?"

Celeste had excused herself at that point and went to powder her nose.

"You work at shipyard, *da*?" he asked.

"Yeah, sometimes though I usually work in the dockyard. Why""

"As electrician."

"That's right. How'd ya know that?"

"Don't matter. All that matters is I pay money...good money for some information." He reached inside his jacket, pulled out an envelope and set it in the middle of the table.

"Whaddya sayin'?"

He shrugged his shoulders then said, "You clever man. You understand."

"Jesus," Mitchell swore, realizing what the Russian was suggesting. He leaned forward and lowered his voice, saying, "You want me to steal...?"

"*Nyet*," Petrov said, shaking his head. "We only interested to learn new, um, ways my country can defend itself. Your government is being stupid in not sharing with mine. We are allies, da?"

"Yeah, I 'spose so," he said, as he glanced inside the envelope and saw a neat stack of banknotes. He lifted the edge of the envelope flap with a finger and saw that the notes were all twenties; he estimated there had to be almost two hundred dollars there. He swallowed hard.

"So?" Petrov said, staring at him. "Think what you can buy for your woman?"

Since Celeste came into his life, he had been spending a lot of his savings on her, to the point where he was beginning to run low. He was afraid that once his money ran out his time with her would be over. It never occurred to him to see her for what she was or what she was doing to him. The only thoughts in his mind were of the nights of unbridled sex and the looks of envy whenever they were out together.

"What kind 'a information do you want?" he finally asked, looking up from the money.

"I let you know later," Petrov said, taking the envelope back. He fished out two of the banknotes and pushed them with a finger across the table to Mitchell. "Think of this as, how you say, a down payment."

Mitchell took the banknotes and stuffed them in his shirt pocket, unaware of the slight shift of Petrov's eyes. Then suddenly, Celeste was back and she sat down beside him, placing a hand on the inside of his leg and gently squeezing it.

"You work for me now, understand." Petrov looked from him to the woman who was smiling at him.

Larry Mitchell suddenly realized he had been neatly set up and taken in. That was almost a month ago. It was not long after that night when he learned how he was setup. It turned out that Dumont was in fact Petrov's mistress and that she fingered Larry for the Russian. And yet, as angry as he felt, he still could not give her up. She was like a powerful drug, and he was addicted to her. In the end he turned traitor but only if he could still bed her. She agreed. It seemed she liked how he was in bed.

Now here he was standing in the shadows on a freezing night waiting to sell secrets to the Russian.

He finally spotted Petrov rounding the corner at the end of the street and headed to where he stood waiting.

"You have something?" Petrov asked, stepping into the shadowed area next to him.

"Yeah," Mitchell said, reaching inside his jacket and pulling out a sealed envelope. He passed it to him.

"Near 's I can tell it's an update on the sonar they're usin'."

"Good," the Russian said, putting the envelope inside his coat. He extracted another packet and slipped it to him: his thirty pieces of silver. Larry hated what he was doing but didn't care. All that mattered was keeping her.

"Next time I need whatever you can get on their radar," Petrov said, breaking in on his thoughts.

"I don't know 'bout that."

"Try."

"It ain't so easy. Some places I simply can't get into, understand?"

"Try," Petrov said again, this time a bit more insistently. Mitchell sometimes felt there was something threatening behind it.

"Look, I'm jus' an electrician, see, not an electronics specialist. The security people will catch onto me."

"You find a way, da. I pay you extra hundred dollars."

"It ain't the money, fer Chrissake. I'm tryin' ta tell ya, I can't get into the buildin' where the information is kept."

"Then find me someone who can."

Mitchell's mind was racing, trying to think who he could approach then it hit him" Jack Markham.

"I think I might know someone," he said.

* * *

Lieutenant Commander Michael Parks was a young twenty-three-year-old First Lieutenant when he arrived in Canada in nineteen thirty-eight as part of a joint committee to discuss the current situation in Europe, and Canada's role in the event of war with Germany. His superiors soon discovered his talents and ability for organizing complex operations, such as setting up the security measures for the convoy system they knew would be needed. It was then they decided to post him to the port city of Halifax, Nova Scotia where, as in the first war, the city was to serve as the primary convoy staging port.

Parks was an intelligent man, amiable with an easy-going manner that put people at ease around him. All good attributes which had served him well since his arrival. He quickly established himself in his new role and as quickly gained the respect of those working under him. He was also the subject of much interest among the single female staffers, both military and civilian. Unfortunately for them, he did not appear to have much interest in making any overtures in that regard. It would have a mistake to think he did not like women, quite the contrary, but the job at hand left no room for those sorts of distractions. In a short time, he distinguished himself and within a couple of years he was promoted to Lieutenant Commander and head of Naval Intelligence operations in the port.

During the last four years he had dealt with numerous attempts by the German intelligence service, the Abwehr, to infiltrate the port. In his endeavor to keep them at bay he had help from a Royal Canadian Mounted Police officer, Phillip Mulroney and, on several occasions, Detective John Robichaud and his partner, Pete Duncan, of the city police. This team proved to be exceptionally adept in their respective areas, making his job so much easier. Which was a good thing, he thought, as he sat at his desk looking down at the document stamped SECRET in red ink. It had just been delivered by special courier.

He tore open the seal and extracted the documents inside. He read through them twice, as he always did to make sure he understood the contents. Then setting them down, he reached for the telephone on his desk and lifted the handset, holding the secure telephone close against his ear. When the in-house operator answered he asked the female operator to connect him to Captain Ansell in Ottawa. Ansell was his immediate superior at the National Command Centre in Ottawa.

"Yes sir, one moment, please." A few moments later he heard a man's voice in his ear.

"Ansell, "he said.

"Parks here, sir. I just received the report. That is why I am calling. What is it exactly you want me to do? I mean, the Russians are our allies, are they not?"

"Yes," the man said. "They are, however, as you have read in the report that MI5 has forwarded, a confidential dossier has been compiled. In it they detail Stalin's efforts to obtain military secrets, particularly pertaining to radar, sonar, and weapons. They have also learned that the Russian secret service, called SMERSH or NKVD, has dispatched cells to allied countries, namely, Britain, the U.S. and us to try and get the information."

"I see. I take it that it is the British position that they should not have access to that information?"

"More or less, yes, that is correct and as such, it is also the position shared by our government. Based what they know and what we have been uncovering here, it is their opinion that the Communists will likely become a major political issue once this show is over and they don't want to give them any edge to use against us. According to our sources, a Russian named, Nikolai Petrov has been identified as a possible NKVD agent and was last reported heading your way. He may be traveling with his mistress, a suspected Quebec Separatist. Her presence raises other questions and concerns, so please get them before they do any harm."

"I thought you said she was his mistress?"

"That is correct," Ansell said. "However, we know she has a criminal history with the Quebec Police as an agitator, stirring up unrest and opposition within the labour force and anti-war factions. She also has a history of violence."

"Again, I must ask, what is it you want me to do, exactly?"

"First, find out if they are in your area. Once you have that, you will put them under surveillance and monitor who they contact; the usual sort of thing you have been doing dealing with the Germans. I cannot emphasis it enough when I say that this comes from the top, understand?"

"Yes sir," Parks said. "Completely."

"Good," he said. "I knew I could rely on you."

"A question, if I may?"

"Yes?"

"What am I to do if I find them engaged in stealing our secrets?"

"As far as I am concerned...arrest them and report back directly to me. I will alert the appropriate agencies with a stake in this matter."

"And if these people choose to not come peacefully?"

"You are authorized to take whatever measures you deem necessary. I need not remind you that the NKVD has a long history of using extreme measures in their pursuits. So use extreme caution and be prepared."

"Yes sir, of course. You do understand that if and when we find these people that any confrontations could lead to a serious political situation as I am sure you can appreciate."

"We will deal that situation here in Ottawa if it arises. For now, just find them if they are present and neutralize them. This is a priority assignment. Use whatever resources available to you. We want this matter settled as quickly as is practical."

"Yes sir," Parks said. "I will attend to it immediately."

"Oh. One more thing," the man said. "You will contact me directly on the secure line with daily updates, is that clear?"

"Yes sir, understood. Is that all?"

"For the moment. You will be brief on any information as it becomes available."

"Sir. Thank you." With that the line went dead and he hung up the phone.

After several minutes considering what he was told and its ramifications, he reached for the phone again and dialed three numbers. The call was answered on the first ring.

"Mulroney," the voice on the other end said.

Phil. Can you spare me a few minutes?"
"Sure. When?"
"Now."

Chapter Two

The squad room was unusually quiet, even at this hour. Two plainclothes detectives sat at their respective desks writing up shift reports. They looked tired. It had been a busy night. Tired was the norm these days.

It was now the fourth year of the war. Halifax had undergone rapid changes as it struggled to cope with the strains and stresses as the primary staging port for the convoys taking supplies of materials, fuel, and men to England for deployment to Europe and the fight with Germany. The pressures on the civilian population were, at times, pushed to the breaking point. The deprivations, profiteering and resentments from the men in uniform about how they were being treated as well as the merchantmen was nearing the boiling point. But they were resilient and managed to make it through every day in spite of the food, gas and housing shortages imposed by rationing.

Unfortunately, cracks had been on the rise lately spilling over into the open that kept the local police force busy. These ranged from the occasional protests from the small groups of anti-war protesters and other malcontents, demanding government changes to the animosity between locals and the merchant seamen, sailors and foreigners that roamed the streets looking for anything to alleviate the stresses of the North Atlantic crossings. It was hard to recall a time when the city lockup was empty.

I had submitted a report to my boss, Captain Danial Morrison, warning of the growing tensions from the government's restrictions on alcohol to the rampant price gouging by merchants and especially landlords, and that these factors must be considered in conjunction with the numbers of idle servicemen with no place to go. Everyone was tired of the war and constant demands, and abuses, that weighed heavily on the city, not least on the force whose responsibility it was to maintain order.

My name is John Robichaud. I am the lead detective with the Halifax Police Department. I am originally from Cape Breton where I was born into a mix marriage; my mother was a Mi'kmaq. I left when I was fifteen and headed for the United States where I enlisted in the infantry and shipped out for Europe. After the war ended, I was returned to the States and discharged. A friend I made while in service convinced me to head for Boston where he lived. We both ended up on the Boston Police Force. I soon discovered I liked being a cop and did well. A few years later, I learned that my father was very ill and left for home. He died soon after I returned.

It did not take long before I realized I could not live there anymore, so saying goodbye to my mother for a second time, I headed for Halifax where I was soon working as a cop again. That was in nineteen twenty-four. A year later I met and married my wife and now I have a family with three children: two boys and a girl.

Halifax was a grubby and drab city-port which meant it was also a rough place. It was also a WASP city (White Anglo-Saxon Protestant): the English controlled every aspect of life – commerce, government, religion, education, so much so that the city was clearly divided into them, the British, and the others. It did not help that the British and pro-British made no effort to conceal their contempt or bias against the non-English, especially the French. This made for some difficult policing at times, particularly when you threw the military presence into the mix. It was an education being a beat cop in those early days, luckily I had my experiences as a Boston cop in similar circumstances with the Irish community there to draw on.

In due course, I proved my worth and value and was promoted to detective.

I was sitting at my desk, reading the daily paper and enjoying a mug of coffee before starting my day, as was my usual custom. The war news out of England was much improved these days since the Americans had finally come into the fray. The beachheads of D-Day had been consolidated, allowing for the Allies to make significant advances toward freeing France. It looked like Italy was about to fall as well, and the Germans were retreating from Greece. Peace, once a distant hope, looked like it could be possible...at long last. I for one was more than ready; I had my fill of the war and was bone tired.

Just at that moment I sensed someone come into the room behind me. I had a good idea who it was.

"Mornin'," I said, folding the paper and setting it down on the desk. I turned in my seat and looked at my partner, Pete Duncan.

"Mornin'," he replied, sounding tired and angry. He hung up his overcoat and hat then went to pour a mug of coffee.

"Bad night?" I asked.

"Could say that." He waved at the two men who waved back as he went to his desk and sat down. "I was on-call. Got a call at two this mornin'. A domestic disturbance down on Bland Street."

"I'm guessin' it wasn't, judgin' by the look of you."

"Turned out to be some sailors were mixin' it up with a landlady's ole man an' some a' his drinkin' pals. Seems one a' the sailors was rentin' a room from the woman an' was tryin' to bring his mates in so they could get some sleep but she wasn't havin' any a' that unless they coughed up ten bucks apiece. Anyway, the lads had jus' come back from an escort an' been to a nearby pig an' were a bit tight an' took exception. I called for a coupla more uniforms to help out as well as the Shore Patrol."

"I can guess the rest," I said. "Where are the sailors an' the others?"

"The SP guys took the sailors away an' I tossed the others in the cells."

"Any of our people hurt?"

"No, jus' the usual; a few bruises. One a' the uniforms might have a shiner."

"Well, that's somethin'. Look, why doncha head home for a few hours. It doesn't look like there's a lot goin' on right now," I said.

"You sure?" Pete said. "I mean, I'm good to..."

"I'm sure. If something comes up an' I need you, I'll call. Now get outta here." I checked the wall clock: it read, seven-fifteen. "I'll see you after lunch."

"Thanks, Robie. I really appreciate this."

He stood up and put his overcoat back on and grabbed his hat.

"Take a car," I said as he started for the door.

He picked a set of keys off the pegboard on the wall and nodded.

The call from my boss, Captain Morrison, came an hour and a half later.

Morrison has been the head of the police operations since before the war in thirty-nine. He was a Lieutenant up till this last summer when the city council decided to add more manpower to the force and promote both him and me; him to Captain and me to Lieutenant. Pete also got a boost to full Sergeant. I was happy for him since he and Aggie, his wife, recently had a baby and another on the way.

I knocked on the glass panel of the door as I opened it and stepped inside.

"What's up?" I asked as I took my usual chair in front of his desk.

He was a big man in his early fifties. Like me, he had been a cop most of his adult life, starting out as a patrolman walking a beat, paying his dues and earning his stripes to finally attain his current position as Chief of Police. We developed a strong friendship over the years based on mutual respect and trust.

"Just got off the phone with the mayor," he said in his usual direct manner.

"Uh-oh," I said, knowing that this didn't bode well for me. Usually when he calls me up after such a call it means that I'm in for something serious.

"Yeah. He got off a call from your old pal Parks down at Naval Intelligence. Seems he's got himself a situation that needs your particular touch. He asked that you and Pete be seconded to his department to assist them on a highly sensitive matter and since both of you have security clearance, the mayor agreed."

"He give any idea what it's about?"

"None." Morrison shook his head. "I assume you'll be put in the picture after you get there. You and Pete have anything pressing on your desks at the moment?"

"Nothing that can't wait or be shoveled off to one of the other men. Mostly it's dealin' with the tensions in the city between civilians and the mariners, mostly the navy."

"A blind man should have seen this problem coming. The Council and the Provincial Government took too long to crack down on all this profiteering, and the Navy," he said disgustedly, "they should have been more sympathetic to the plight of their own."

"No argument from me. So, when do they want us down there?"

"Today."

"Crap," I said. "Pete was on call last night an' got called out 'round two o'clock. It was supposed to be a domestic disturbance abut turned out to be a dispute

31

with some sailors an' a landlady. It got messy. I sent him home for a coupla hours sleep."

"That's okay," he said. "After lunch will be soon enough. You and him can head down to the headquarters building this afternoon. Check in and let me know how long they plan on keeping there if you can."

'Sir," I said, standing up. I recognized the tone of voice he used to signal the meeting was over.

I made my way back to the squad room thinking about the situation in the city. I knew that the pressure was nearing the breaking point. It was bad enough that men came looking for work, but many made the mistake of bringing their families, wives, and girlfriends, especially the sailors only to find no place to live, and made to feel they were not welcome.

Another problem we had to contend with was the frustration among the men who served on the ships, both military and merchant, who survived the crossings and returned to a 'dry' city with not many amenities to ease the stress. This ended up giving rise to the number of illegal boozers and bootleggers that sold liquor, sometimes homemade and unsafe to drink.

By the time I reached my desk I was feeling pissed off and tired. Maybe this assignment would be just what I needed to get my footing back.

Pete arrived back at one-thirty, looking a lot better for the rest.

"Feelin' better" I asked.

"Yeah," he said, starting to remove his overcoat. "Thanks."

"Don't bother. We off."

"Oh? What's up?"

"Parks. Looks like he needs our help?"

"What, again? Sometimes I think he sees us as some kind a section of the Intelligence Corps."

"Seems that way," I said with a chuckle. "Well, it'll give us a break from the crap we've been dealin' with lately."

I picked up my phone and called Lieutenant Commander Michael Parks' direct line.

"Lieutenant Commander Parks line," I woman said.

"Oh, I thought this was his direct line?" I said. "Is he not there?"

"This is his line. He has stepped away from his desk for a few moments, who is calling, please?"

"Sorry. Detective Robichaud from the..."

"Oh, yes. Of course, Detective. I believe he has been expecting your call. Shall I get him?"

"No, that's okay. Jus' let him know that I'm headin' down there now with Detective Duncan and' should be there in about twenty minutes."

"Yes sir. I will get this to him immediately."

"Thank you," I said then hung up.

"Ready?" I said to Pete as I grabbed my overcoat and hat.

"After you," he said as we headed for the stairs that would take us up to the parking area in the Grand Parade ground.

Naval Headquarters was located down at the south end of Barrington Street in a building commandeered early in the war by the Navy League. This was where much of the business of the port was run from and, as well as being the base of intelligence operations, it was also where most of the convoy operations were done in the basement.

When we arrived and cleared the security area in the lobby, we were escorted to Parks' office where an attractive young WAVE dressed in the standard black uniform of the navy greeted us and then put us in his office, saying he would be along shortly. She also wore the half gold ring on her jacket sleeve of a Sub-lieutenant. She offered us coffees, which we accepted.

"Ah, Robie. Pete," how good it is to see you both again," Parks said when he entered his office, offering his hand in a warm and genuine handshake. We came to know each other very well over the course of the last three years and had become friends.

Not far behind him came his constant shadow and unofficial second in command

34

of the intelligence unit, Inspector Phil Mulroney of the Royal Canadian Mounted police on permanent assignment to Halifax attached to Naval Intelligence. He pulled a chair over next to me and sat down.

Phil was a big man in his early forties with a pleasant personality and easy-going manner. He was also intelligent and had a keen mind for intelligence work. He too, was a friend, particularly with Pete since they were close in temperament and age.

"So, what's up?" I asked, grinning. "Someone steal a ship?"

"Not quite, but not too far from the mark," Parks said, smiling back.

"Huh?"

"The reason you and Pete have been sent down is two-fold. First, you both have been cleared and granted high enough security clearances, and second, we once again need your well proven investigative skills."

Pete and I sat there listening, waiting for the other shoe to drop.

"Right. As you probably know from the news reports, censored though they may be by our good friend Mr. Murray, the situation in Europe seems to have finally begun to turn in our favour. Well, I can tell you now...they have turned. Hitler has made a number of serious blunders in the last year, not the least being his opening a second front with Russia. Also, we got lucky on D-Day by successfully diverting the Nazi's attention away from Normandy."

"So does that mean the war's almost over?" Pete asked.

"Not quite," Parks said, "but the end is sight."

"I take it that is not why we're here," I cut in.

"Correct. I was contacted by my superiors in Ottawa in the last twelve hours. It appears that a report was sent from our sources in Britain, alerting us to the possibility of Russian spy cells being sent to Allied countries with orders to obtain any information of recent technological developments, particularly in the areas of radio, radar, and weapons."

"Why would they send spies here?" Pete asked. "Aren't 'spose to be our allies and friends?"

"Out of necessity only. Stalin has made his views and aims as to democracy quite clear. But that is a matter to be dealt with from other sectors, thankfully. Our main concern is to first determine if such a cell is in fact here and then neutralize it."

"Again, why here?" Pete pressed.

"The information they are after is mostly used on board our naval ships," Phil said, speaking for the first time. "And Halifax is the largest port on the Eastern seaboard north of any American port. Plus, we have a major ship repair facility."

"Exactly," Parks said. "This would be the ideal location for these people to gather information."

"Okay," I said. "I get that. But surely your people are better equipped to deal with these people."

"Normally, yes. But since the turn of our fortunes overseas there has been an increased demand for experienced command level personnel, especially in the intelligence area. We are, once again, caught with a major problem without adequate personnel. And you and Pete have proven yourselves to be so very good at what you do. What we need, I need, is people like you two who know the city and can operate outside the official and political arenas."

"In other words, we can step on toes you can't...or won't," I said.

"Just so," he said.

"So, what is it exactly you want from us, although I can make a good guess?"

He smiled wryly as he went on. "Once we have more information, which is forthcoming, I want you to begin a search for these people. We do not know how many there will be or even if they will be only males. However, we do know that these cells are always comprised of members of the Russian secret service, usually from an organization called, SMERSH."

"What in the name of God is a SMERSH?" Pete asked.

"We do not know too much about them, but they have a separate division, or directorate as they call it, called the NKVD. These are manned by people devotedly loyal to the Communist Party."

"Oh, one more thing we know, they are ruthless in their practices and deadly. They will not hesitate to kill if necessary to achieve their goal," Phil added.

"Great," I said.

"It gets a little more complicated, I'm afraid," Parks said.

"It usually does," I said, looking back at him. "Let's have it."

"Unlike our past dealings with agents, this time there is a political element that has to be considered."

"Meaning?"

"We have to be very careful when apprehending them once we find them."

"How careful?" I asked.

"Careful."

"An' what if they won't cooperate, uh, nicely?" Pete asked.

Parks and Phil looked at each other for a moment as let the question hang between them.

"I see," I said. "Well, I promise you this Michael, we won't shoot anyone unless they shoot first."

"Agreed and understood. I trust your judgment as always. Well. that about covers all I had to say on the matter for the present. I will now leave you with Phil who will go over everything we have at the moment. He will be your direct link to this office while you are working on the file. Every resource we have will be at your disposal as usual. Good luck and... thank you, again."

We all stood up and Pete and I shook hands with him then followed Phil down the hall to a small meeting room. Inside there was a wooden table laden with about a half dozen files and a couple of boxes. There was a smaller table with a hotplate and kettle on it and several mugs. Pete and I dropped our overcoats over the backs of our chairs and sat down.

"You and Pete will work from here. My phone line will be manned twenty-four hours a day in case you need anything. My office is across the hall. This room will be secured whenever we are not using it. Only you, Pete and I will have a key to the door."

"Jesus, that's a lot of precautions," I said, impressed by the steps they were taking. "Jus' who the hell are we dealin' with?"

"Like Michael said, they are probably Communist Party loyalists working with their secret service. Unfortunately, we are only now starting to learn about that department. But what we do know isn't good. There've been reports coming out of Europe, particularly the Eastern Front and the Caucuses of atrocities and other things that are being done by this NKVD."

"So, it's true what I've been hearin' 'bout Stalin bein' a dictator of sorts," I said.

"Looks like it. Remember the news reports back in the nineteen-eighteen about the Bolsheviks assassinating the Tsar and his entire family. But none of that concerns us now. Our task is to try and find out if one of their cells is here and stop what they're up to."

"I don't get it," Pete said. "They're 'spose to be our allies, right? So why do they need to steal whatever they're here for? We don't share anymore?"

"All I can tell you," Phil said, sitting down, "is the political situation with Stalin has never been a good one. Ever since he took over from Lenin, he has been pushing a political agenda that runs against everything the other countries believe. In fact, it some circles, many think when this war is over, he's going to be the next big threat. The common attitude is that if it hadn't been for Hitler and Germany starting this war, the western countries would probably be facing off against Russia as they have made no secret that they intend to bring Europe under the Soviet system."

"And now they want to make sure they don't get their hands on our secrets to use against us when this war is over, is that it?"

"Couldn't have said it any simpler than that myself."

"I got a question for you, Phil. I understand your people have your own ways of handlin' these situations, but we're street cops, an' don't handle them the same way or by the same rules."

"Your point being?" Phil said.

"My point is, what do we do if we find them an' get dragged into somethin' if they choose to not come along quietly?"

"First, you're here precisely because you are cops. We don't have the authority to operate in, what is clearly, your jurisdiction. And, second, as of right now they aren't enemies, so we can't take any actions against them. But if they are here to steal our secrets then as far as we are concerned, they are enemies. Having said that, our hands are still tied somewhat but not yours. Our thinking is that you can go after them."

"On what charge?" I asked. "They haven't committed any crimes as far as I can see."

"If they acquire any secret documents then they are in possession of stolen property, yes?"

"That sound like you're graspin' at straws."

"It's the best we came up with in lieu of dealing with them as enemy agents."

"Hmmm. Not bad. I suppose we could make a case by goin' at it from another direction."

"What're you thinking?" Phil asked.

"Let's say we hear somethin', say from an anonymous source, reporting somethin' suspicious..."

"Like maybe from someone, say, in the shipyard," he said, cutting me off.

I nodded, saying, "...or from someone inside Naval Intelligence."

"Then you'd be obliged to look into it and one thing could lead to another. You really are a devious bugger, aren't you?"

"When the occasion calls for it," I said, smiling.

"Right. I suggest we keep this strictly 'in-house'. Only the four of us will communicate anything to do with the investigation between ourselves until we have something watertight to act on. Agreed?"

"Agreed," I said.

Pete nodded.

"Good, that's settled, at this point you can exercise your own judgment on how to handle whatever situation arises."

"Jus' so I'm clear, if we find them an' they choose to not cooperate, we can go as far as arrestin' them? Even though they are allies?" Pete asked.

Yes, that's correct."

"Won't that create some sort of political problem for the mayor an' us?"

"We don't think so. It is the general view that if they are here on a spying mission for their government, they will not want to be compromised and will disavow any knowledge of their being here. So, if and when you do find them, we will look at our options at that time."

"Okay," I said. "Now what?"

"Now we wait. Michael is in constant contact with his people in Ottawa who are on this. Once they have any additional information about these cells, especially if one is en route to here or is here, they will alert him. For now, you and Pete will have to bide your time."

"Here?" Pete asked.

"Yeah, unless you have to get back to the station," Phil said, nodding.

"No, we're good," I said. "Morrison cut us loose until you're done."

"Excellent. May as well get right to it. I've arranged to put together what we got any Russians in the city. Mostly, they are merchantmen, although, there are also several civilians here as liaisons for their government's Embassy in Ottawa; translators mostly."

"Do you have any background information on this group, what did you called it...?"

"SMERSH," Pete said, cutting in.

"Not a lot," Phil answered. "Michael is on to Ottawa to get any information from Special Branch and even the FBI in the States. He thinks we'll have something fairly soon; we just have to wait."

"Someday someone has to come up with a better way to share information between all the agencies an' police," I said.

"Now that would be something," Phil said with a wry smile.

As it turned out, we didn't have to wait long.

Chapter Three

Larry Mitchell sat at a table in the Halifax Shipyards worker's canteen eating his lunch: a plate of corned beef hash, two slices of freshly made bread and a large mug of strong tea. If nothing else, the Yard made sure its workers were well fed. Normally he would be enjoying a meal like this, especially the corned beef hash, but today he sat there distracted, picking away at the food. He had a lot on his mind and none of it good.

He was waiting for someone.

"Hey, Larry," a man said from behind him. "How's the chow?"

"Huh?" he said, turning to look at Jack Markham as stood beside him. "Tuesday. Corned beef."

"Good. Hang on a minute while I go get me a plate. Be right back."

He watched as Markham went to the steam table where they were serving the food.

Larry met him about a year ago at some boozer's place and they struck up a conversation. It turned out he and Markham had a lot in common. They were both in their twenties, single and liked the same things: drinking, loose women, and gambling. The big difference between them turned out to be Markham's compulsive need to gamble, especially on poker, that, and his interest in teenage girls.

A few months after they met, they were at a card game and he had a very bad night, losing a couple a hundred dollars and had to lay down a marker. This ended with him getting into a jam with the people who ran the game. Mitchell helped to bail him out which was okay because the amount was not that high, and he always paid him back.

Markham came to Halifax looking for work. Within days he landed a job at the shipyards, however, once it became known that he was a certified technician he was transferred over to the naval dockyard in their radiography department. This was where they worked on sonar and radar equipment. He signed on as an electrical technician maintaining the sonar and radar machines sets.

Mitchell soon learned that his new friend managed to land this job without having to go through the usual security clearances he had to endure when he was hired. Which, in hindsight, was a lucky break for him because if the security people learned about his gambling and sexual preferences he probably would have been sent back to Ontario as a security risk.

Larry kept watching his friend as he finished paying the cashier then walked back to the table and sit down.

"So? Whazzup?" he said, reaching for the salt shaker.

"How'd ya like to make some extra dough, ya know, on the down 'n low?" Mitchell asked in a low voice as he leaned forward.

"You kiddin'? Yeah, I'm interested. You know me. I can always use extra dosh."

"I kinna figured as much."

"How?"

"Not here," Mitchell said, sitting back. "Too many ears. Later; after work. Let's meet up at Sampson's place an' talk."

"Sounds good to me. But it'll hafta ta be after eight o'clock. I got tapped to stay on to work on a rush job."

"No problem. Eight's fine."

They finished eating then went their separate ways until later.

Dave Sampson was a local bootlegger selling beer and liquor out of his kitchen. He also ran a floating poker game in the basement. Sometimes on weekends, he ran a couple of women from his upstairs bedrooms.

Mitchell arrived at Sampson's place on Agricola Street around seven-thirty. He recognized the few people sitting around drinking as regulars: mostly labourers or other workmen who probably lived in the neighbourhood in for their evening beer.

There were no women around tonight and likely would not be since it was a week night. The women were locals looking to make extra money to supplement their ration stamps. They were mostly in their thirties, not bad looking and clean. Mitchell suspected they were married, and their husbands were either in the navy or on one of the merchant ships. It did not matter either way to him as long as they put out and he got his money's worth, at least that was all he needed before he met Celeste.

Markham showed up at quarter past eight, He looked tired. When he saw Mitchell he waved then went and bought a quart of beer.

"You look like shit," I said.

"That ass hole in the lab rode me pretty hard," he said, sitting down. "One a these days..."

He was referring to his supervisor, Ken Lawrence. A stuffed shirt with a high regard for himself. Liked putting on airs and was a know-it-all according to Jack. A real pain in the ass. Always sucking up to the bosses, taking credit for any good work done by the others.

"So? You said somethin' 'bout makin' extra money?" he said as he poured a glass of beer. "It's not anythin" illegal, is it?"

"Does it really matter?" Mitchell answered.

"Not much."

"So that mean you're interested?"

"Yeah. I could use the extra money. I been on a losin' streak lately. Whatta I gotta do?"

"There's this fella looking for information..." I started to say.

"Whoa," Jack said, putting up a hand. "I ain't no traitor."

"It's not like that, this guy's a Russkie; an ally."

"An ally? So, why's he looking for information here? Can't he get right from the source, I mean, if he is really an ally?"

"Somethin' 'bout too much politics between his government an' the others. Anyway, he sez his government jus' wants to get information so they can defend themselves after the war is over."

"Let me guess, they want to know what we got for radar?"

"An' sonar an' radio, ya know, any a technical stuff."

"So how'd you get connected with him?"

"Celeste put us together. I've been gettin' him bits an' pieces but he needs the real information, ya know, the stuff you have access to. He pays pretty good."

"How good?"

"He's paid me between forty an' a hundred bucks a shot so far. But I'd wager he'd cough up a lot more for what you can bring."

"Jesus," Markham said, topping up his glass.

"So, you interested?" Mitchell asked.

"I reckon there'd be no harm in talkin' to the guy."

"Okay. I'll set up a meetin' an' get back to ya. Another beer?"

"Yeah, thanks."

Mitchell got up and went to the kitchen and bought two quarts pale ale, brewed locally by Keith's Brewery.

* * *

Nikolai Petrov lay propped up against a pillow smoking a cigarette, feeling satisfied and content. His thoughts went back to another cold November in nineteen-forty-three. He was standing at attention in front of a large oak desk in a room inside the Lubyanka Building in Moscow. He had been ordered to present himself to the Deputy Head of the NKVD for a special assignment.

He was a Junior Lieutenant of State Security in the NKVD assigned to the Special Assignments Directorate which handled the numerous espionage activities both domestic and foreign. He had been transferred here mainly because he spoke English and was a dedicated and loyal Party member. It also did not hurt his promotion that he had a reputation for being thoroughly ruthless in performing his assignments.

At that meeting, his superior instructed him that he was to be part of a series of teams being sent out of Russia to the Allied countries where he was to recruit people who could provide Russia with secret information on the various developments being used by their respective military forces. His particular assignment was in Halifax, Nova Scotia in Canada; the primary staging port for the U.S. and Canadian navies as well as the convoys.

He was given prepared papers and the names of his contacts as well a packet with a thousand dollars in Canadian banknotes. He was to leave immediately for the port of Arkhangelsk and report on board a Russian transport due to sail for the United States in four days. Upon his arrival, he was to report to the Embassy there for further instructions.

When he finally arrived in New York, he jumped ship and made his way to the embassy as ordered where his handler then gave him the rest of his orders. His cover was to be a Russian Liaison for the Soviet merchant ships and crews arriving in the port. His orders were to also ensure that there were no defections by the seamen and to use any force he deemed necessary to dissuade them, even executions. He was given a new set of papers and additional cash. His contact then arranged for him to take the train north to Quebec City where he would make contact with a local woman who would go to Halifax with him as his assistant. She was not Russian but supported the Soviet cause. She agreed to provide whatever service required of her.

Three days later he found himself in Quebec City, Canada, where he made contact with the woman who was to go with him.

He let his eyes drift down to look at the young woman laying naked beside him on the bed, enjoying the sensation of her breast pressing against the side of his chest and her hand as it slid lower over his abdomen. The woman was insatiable, he thought with a smile.

He learned she was part of a radical revolutionary separatist group fighting for independence from Canada. At the moment, she was part of a protest against the federal government's reneging on their conscription policy. She had been responsible for several arson attacks and assaults against the Provincial police.

He was taken by her devotion and ardour to her cause, that, and the fact she was also a beauty and young. Not long after he approached her, they were in bed together and had been lovers since then. He soon learned of her appetite for sex and a willingness to use it in his cause.

"How much longer do I have to sleep with that man?" she asked softly without looking up.

"Stop whenever you want," he answered. "I have him now."

"Good. He is becoming wearisome." Which was her way of saying Mitchell no longer interested her carnally. "We have much work to do, and I want to be of help."

"Ah, my pet, you will be."

He eased himself lower under the blanket, rolling on to his side as he embraced her. Oh yes, my pet, you will be, he thought as he leaned in and kissed her.

Later, he stood in front of the washstand studying his reflection in the mirror as he shaved. He paused mid-stroke when he heard the phone ring in the hall. Odd, he thought, who would be calling here? This was a safe house procured by the Embassy in Ottawa and at the moment he was the only person staying in the house. No one except for the woman, who lay sleeping in the other room and Larry Mitchell, knew this number.

He put the razor down and went out into the hall to answer the phone. He hooked the phone between two fingers and lifted it off the small side table. It was one of the old candlestick models.

"Yes?" he said, into the mouthpiece as he held the receiver to his ear.

"It's me," Mitchell said.

"I know. What do you want?"

"I have somebody who's interested in what we talked about."

"Meet me same place with your friend at eight o'clock tonight."

"Eight, right. By the way, have ya seen Celeste? She wasn't at work today."

"Nyet, er, no."

"Alright, fergit it. See ya at eight."

Petrov hung the receiver back on its hook and set the phone down. He turned and went back into the bedroom where Celeste was sitting up against the headboard, her bare chest with those beautiful breasts exposed for him to see.

"Something come up?" she asked, looking at him with those blue eyes.

"Da," he said. "Mitchell has found someone who wants to talk."

"Bon. When?"

"Tonight."

"Do you need me to come along?"

"Nyet. I can manage. Mitchell did say he was looking for you."

"*Merde*. The man is insatiable. All he wants is sex."

"I understand why," he said with a knowing smile.

"Oh you," she said, tossing a pillow at him. The action made her breasts shake causing him to laugh a little.

"Oh pet, do not be angry. It was meant as a compliment. Now get up. I have a matter to see to."

The day before he received a package in the post from his handler in Ottawa. Inside were items of clothing inside which were sewn secret coded messages. One of these messages told him to investigate a report of an anti-Soviet group operating in Halifax. This group reportedly has been assisting sailors on Russian merchant ships to defect; if true, then he was to take steps to shut them down.

A tall order he thought after decoding the message. After all, he was only one man. But, if there was one man who could do this, it was him.

"You are looking deep in thought, *mon amour*," Celeste said as she emerged from the bedroom. She was dressed in her work smock, a pink knee length article with a wraparound tie at the waist.

"I have some business I must see to," Petrov said, turning to look at her.

"Anything I can help with?"

"Perhaps. I must see what it is first."

She crossed over to him in her bare feet and threw her arms around his neck, rising up on her tiptoes, she kissed him lightly on the lips.

"Let me know." She let him go and went to put on her shoes. "I have to work today, but I can leave anytime."

"I know," he said, smiling. "Will you be coming here tonight?"

"I see no reason why not, unless Mitchell turns up." She gave him a questioning look.

"It is still best I keep him under control."

"I understand," she said with just a hint of disappointment in her voice.

"Soon. We will no longer need him, then..."

"*Oui*?"

"We can leave this dreary city. Now away with you."

Chapter Four

We were still sitting in the room assigned for our use when there a knock on the closed door.

"Yes?" I called out.

The door opened and a young naval rating stepped inside. He wore an anchor over a chevron on his sleeve: a Leading Seaman.

"Detective Robichaud?" he asked, holding the door open.

"That's me," I said, turning in my chair to look at him.

"Sorry, to bother you, but Lieutenant Commander Parks wants to see you right away."

"Why didn't the operator transfer to call here?"

"Don't know, sir. I'm jus' his orderly."

"Okay. Thank you."

"Will that be all, sir?"

"Yeah, thanks."

He spun on his heels and left, closing the door behind him.

"Whaddya think that's all about?" Pete asked.

"Don't know. I'll be right back."

I headed down the hall to Michael's office and knocked on the door as I opened it. There was a pretty young woman dressed in a naval uniform bearing a single light blue ring around the cuff. She was a Sub-lieutenant; a WAVE. She looked up when I stepped in.

"Go right in Detective," she said in a sweet-sounding voice and a smile. "He's expecting you."

I went to the outer door of his office, opened it, went inside, and took a chair.

"You wanted to see me?" I asked.

"Yes, thank you for coming down," he said, putting down his pen. "I just got a call from the Rectory at St. Mary's Basilica. It seems that two Russian brothers somehow arrived on a ship under charter to an American company and have jumped ship here seeking asylum."

"What the hell are they goin' to the church for?" I asked.

"It is not unusual. The church will take in anyone seeking asylum."

"Is that legal?"

"The government's position in this regard is sketchy at best."

"So why call you? I'd a thought this fella would head for a government agency or something like that."

"True. However, I know the Priest who called. He is aware of the fact that I am with Naval Intelligence, so he called for, um, guidance. I called you because of this new business with the Soviets sending a spy cell here and also because this Russian claims that his brother, the other man, was murdered two days ago."

"Murdered?" We haven't heard anythin' about a murder. He sure about this?"

"The Priest seems convinced that something has happened to his brother."

"I'm not sayin' this fella hasn't been killed, might jus' be a case of the body not turnin' up...yet. Think there's a connection?"

"No way to know. But I think we should err on the side of caution, don't you? Perhaps you and Pete could go to the Rectory and have a chat with this man. By the way, it might interest you to know that person makes the fifteenth Russian seaman to jump ship this year."

"I didn't know it was such a problem."

"More than you know," Parks said. "The biggest issue has been dealing with the Soviets in Ottawa. They are insisting that we find them and return them for immediate return to Russia."

"So, what's the problem?"

"We have learned that these men have been summarily executed once they arrive back in Russia. We suspect that some may have been killed on board the returning vessels and their bodies dumped overboard and some may have actually been shot while in custody here in Canada."

"Jesus," I said. "I didn't know it was that bad."

"If even half the reports filtering out of Russia are true, Stalin may be more of villain than Hitler. So, you now see why it is imperative to discover if there is a cell operating here and to shut it down, because I suspect their orders may go beyond the acquisition of our secrets. Remember, most Russian flagged ships call at this port, particularly now with the opening of the Murmansk runs. Mainly because of American attitudes toward Stalin."

"Okay, I get it. What do you want me to do with this fella up at the church?"

"I am not sure, like I said, this is a political matter and not exactly under my purview."

"Well, I can definitely say it isn't under ours."

"I have sent a communique to Ottawa requesting guidance on the matter. One thing is for certain, he cannot stay at the Rectory indefinitely. Too risky. Plus, there is no way to protect him there."

"I suppose we could arrange to take him up to Rockhead."

"That's an option, of course, but it is still no guarantee he would be safe."

"Hm, you're right," I said. "If these people are here, it wouldn't be too hard to get someone inside to take care of him. What about the garrison on the hill?"

I was referring to the army barracks and garrison up at the Citadel. I knew they have a small cell block inside the fortification.

"That is a definite possibility. I will make a call, meanwhile, you and Pete go and have a talk with him. My friend, the Priest, his name is Carl Thompson by the way, says the Russian speaks enough English to make communication possible."

"Right," I said, standing up. "I'll let you know what we find out."

Back in our room, Pete was still pouring through the files. When I came in, he looked up.

"What's up?" he asked.

"Get your coat, we're goin' to church," I said.

"Huh?"

"I'll explain on the way, Let's go."

We arrived at the Basilica Rectory, the house where the clergy lived and conducted church business. It was located next to the church and faced Barrington Street. There was a small parking area between the buildings so I pulled in. We got out and walked around the corner to the main entrance on Barrington.

A woman in her fifties answered the door when I rang the bell. She was heavyset with white hair and wore a frock with an apron over the front. Being a Catholic, I knew she was the housekeeper and cook for the men who lived there; she was probably a member of the Catholic Women's League as well.

"Yes?" she said when she opened the door. "How can I help you?"

"Afternoon," I said, pulling out my identity card and showing it to her. "I'm Detective Robichaud and this here is my partner, Detective Duncan. We're here to see Father Thompson. I think he might be expectin' us."

"Come in." She stepped aside and we entered, removing our hats as we crossed the threshold. "Please. This way."

She led us into an impressive front room. It was furnished with richly upholstered, well-crafted wooden furnishings, a thick pile carpet; heavy drapes hung over the sole window. There were potted plants and bookshelves with plenty of shaded reading lamps placed around the room.

"Please make yourselves comfortable while I call the Father," she said with a wave of her hand then left, closing the door.

"What's that smell?" Pete asked.

"What smell?" I said. "I don't...oh, now I see what you mean. It's nothin'. Most of these places seem to have a distinctive smell to them. I don't know why, maybe it's to do with whatever it is they do in here."

I remembered that Pete was an Anglican Protestant.

A few minutes later the door opened, and a man dressed in a floor length cassock stepped inside.

"Gentlemen," he said, stepping over to us with his hand extended. We stood up. "I'm Father Thompson."

He was young looking with a kind face, although, if you looked closer you would see he was much older than he seemed. He was tall and had a slender build. His black hair was thick and wavy and free of any grey. Overall, not a bad looking fella, I thought, there are some women in the parish who would've liked it if he didn't wear the collar. It occurred to me just then that I didn't recognize him, and I should have since this was my church.

"Detective Robichaud," I said, accepting and shaking his hand. "This is my partner, Detective Duncan." He shook Pete's hand. "Michael Parks has sent us down here to see the Russian seaman who has asked for the sanctuary of church."

"Yes, I know. Michael called. Please sit down."

"You must be new here?" I asked as I sat down. This is my parish an' I..."

"You're right," he said, cutting me off. "I have come down from St. Joseph's up on Russell Street. Father Mitchell called me when the Russian came in, I speak Russian, you see. My grandparents are from a small town called Tula, about eighty or so miles south of Moscow. They emigrated just before the October Revolution in nineteen-seventeen. Michael also told me that you and your partner are not with the Naval Intelligence but are policemen. So, if I may ask, what exactly are your intentions?"

"You're right, we are police officers," I said. "However, we have worked with Michael's agency on a number of occasions since the war started. At the moment we are on detached service again to assist on another matter dealin' with Russians."

"I see. He thinks there may be some connection between what he is doing and this man?"

'Smart fella,' I thought. Quick.

"That's what we're here to try an' figure out, if you'll let us talk to him."

"Yes, of course. Come with me. He's upstairs in one of our rooms."

"By the way," I said as we all stood up. "Has he said anythin' to you since he arrived? I mean, anythin' you can repeat?"

"Funny you should ask," Father Thompson said. "Fortunately, once he learned I spoke Russian, he started to tell me why he was seeking asylum. This way."

He paused a moment, gesturing for us to turn right.

Continuing, he said, "It seems that he and his brother were being sought after back in Russia by the secret police; a group he called, SMERSH. And, before you ask, no, I don't know what that means. Anyway, with the help from like-minded people they were placed on a ship bound for the States. When they arrived here for refueling, they left ship with the captain's help. Somehow, this SMERSH organization found out how they escaped and must have alerted their people in Ottawa who in turn, have dispatched agents to take them into custody."

"Sounds like it is somethin' for the politicians to deal with," Pete said from behind me as we started down the short, darkened hall."

"Maybe so, but when the agent arrived and found out where they were, he showed up and shot one of the brothers. Apparently, they left with knowledge about certain atrocities that Stalin has been perpetrating on his own people.; mostly those who oppose his rule."

"Strange," I said.

"What is?"

"I haven't heard anythin' about this killin'. How long ago did it happen?"

"According to Gregori, that's his name, Gregori Greshenko, this happened two days ago. That's also when he arrived on our doorstep."

"It's possible no one's found the body yet," Pete said when we reached the door to the room.

"He knows you're coming and is willing to cooperate if it means his getting asylum," Father Thompson said, knocking on the door. "I'll leave you to it and wait downstairs."

Gregori Greshenko was sitting on the edge of a single bed, just slightly bigger than a cot. He looked to be about thirty, but I couldn't be sure. He definitely had the Slavic facial features you see in people from that part of the world. He had thick black hair and wore a beard. But it was his eyes that drew your attention most: dark, deep set and full of mistrust, fear, and bad memories.

He was dressed in a pair of heavy woolen pants, a thick shirt and stocking feet. When we came in, he turned and looked at us obviously unsure of what to do.

I removed my overcoat and walked over to a wooden chair and pulled it part way to the bed and sat down.

"My name is John Robichaud," I said, offering my hand. "I am a policeman; a detective. Understand?"

He glanced at my extended hand for a moment before accepting it. He had an incredibly strong grip.

"Greshenko," he said with a thick accent. His eyes darted to Pete who stood behind me still wearing his overcoat.

"That is my partner, another detective. His name is Pete Duncan. Do you know why we are here?"

"Da. Priest tell me you here to talk to me about maybe asylum."

"That's right. But we need to ask you some questions before that happens, understand?"

"Da, er, yes."

"Good." I heard Pete take out his notebook. "First. What ship did you come in on?"

"SS Hudson. I was plotnik, um, how you say...carpenter," he said, making a hammering gesture. "My brother, was uh..." He made shoveling motions.

"A stoker?" I said.

"Da."

"Why did you jump ship here?"

He gave me a funny look.

"Sanctuary. Why?"

"Ah. Russia very bad place now. My brother, Ivan, and me we escape purges."

"I see, what else?'

"We see some things, bad things."

"Like what?"

"Many people shot. All family. We see this and run away."

"Why?"

"We White Russian."

I made a note to find what that meant once we were back at headquarters. I heard the term before but that was it.

"Anythin' else?"

"We see the communist Red Guard take people away dock in trucks."

"Take them where?"

"Gulag, maybe in Siberia. Work as slave labour."

All this was new to me. There was nothing in the papers or on the radio, even with censoring, something like what he was telling us would have slipped out. I was beginning to see why they wanted this man and his brother caught and silenced.

"Tell me about this agent."

"He is communist. He come to ship two days ago. Ivan and me ashore at time. when we got back, Captain, who is friend, tells us someone looking for us. We go to cabin and pack bag then leave ship."

"Where did you go?"

"Captain say we must go to YMCA."

"Is that where he found you?"

"Da," he said. "Ivan, he was out to get food. When he not come back, I go look for him. That when I hear some men talking about someone being shot."

"Then what?" I asked.

"I scared so I leave and come here."

"You Catholic?'

"Nyet. Russian Orthodox. I remember stories this church take people, give sanctuary." He stopped talking and looked from me to Pete then back at me. "You help?"

"Did you see this man?" I asked.

"Nyet...no."

"Alright. I think I have enough for now. We'll be in touch with Father Thompson. For now, you stay here. Don't go outside."

I stood up and put the chair back at the small table. I looked at Greshenko and saw him lower his head, staring at the floor.

Outside the room, Pete and I headed back downstairs.

"Christ, is it really that bad over there?" he asked.

"I reckon so," I said. "I don't know all that much about these communists, but I do remember reading somethin' 'bout their big revolution back in seventeen. As I recall, it was one of the bloodiest since the French Revolution."

We found Father Thompson sitting in the kitchen reading the paper and having a cup of tea.

"Well?" he said, folding the paper and putting it down on the table.

"I'd say he's in a lot of trouble," I said, "if even half of what he said is true."

"It's all true. I am still in touch with some of my family still there and what they tell me about what it's like over there for the people would give you nightmares. What makes me angry, God forgive, is that no one in either government, us or the Americans, seems to want to hear about it or take any action against Stalin."

"The war makes for strange bedfellows," I said. "They must still need their support to end this damn war. Pardon."

He waved a hand and said, "Maybe so, but there has to be an accounting at some point. Anyway, that's politics and doesn't concern this current situation, at least not directly. What are you going to do?"

"I'll report back to Michael and suggest that Greshenko be taken into custody and placed somewhere safe for starters."

"Thanks for that. What about this agent? You think he might try and break in...?"

"It's possible," I said, holding up a hand. "Is there any place you can put him until I can arrange something?"

"For how long?"

"A day, maybe two."

"Hm. It may be possible. Should I let you know where if I can set something up?"

"Yes. I'll make arrangements to have a patrol car on location to keep an eye on him. Jus' make sure it's someplace it'd be hard to get at. Lots of people, that sort a thing. However, call me right away if any trouble comes up."

He thanked us for coming then, after a handshake and a blessing, I suggested to Pete he head back to the station and see what he can find out about the dead brother while I went back to report in with Phil and Michael.

"So? What do think?" Phil asked from across the table in our meeting room. Michel was unavailable for the meeting.

"In my opinion we got us a serious problem here," I said.

"Go on."

"Well, first, I believe this Greshenko fella is genuine and in real danger. As to this agent you think is here, I'd hafta say that no need to guess anymore. It's likely he's already killed someone, this fella's brother."

"What! When?'

"A day ago, accordin' to the priest. Happened somewhere downtown. Pete's at the station to see if there's anything in on the dead man."

"Christ that was fast," Phil said. "How the hell did this agent find him so fast?"

"Probably had local help," I said.

"Who'd have that kind of set up and would work for the Soviets?"

"I can think of one or two." There are always those who have absolutely no scruples or morals when it comes to the evil man does. "As for workin' for the Soviets, hell, these bastards only have one loyalty...money."

"Makes you sick to the stomach, thinking these people exist, damn parasites, the lot of them. If I had my way..."

That was one of few times I ever heard Phil sound so angry. Sometimes I thought he really wasn't cut out to be a cop but then I would remember past dealings and know better.

* * *

The SS Hudson was on approach to the entrance Halifax Harbour. The captain ordered the engine room to reduce speed to slow as he waited for the port pilot to come aboard with the necessary papers to clear the anti-submarine nets protecting the harbour. Once he was on board, he took command of the ship and led it to its berth in Dartmouth at the Imperoyal Refinery where she was booked for refueling.

The Greshenkos left the ship after expressing their gratitude to the captain for his help. They made their way across the harbour and then to the YMCA.

It just gone six o'clock when Ivan Greshenko stepped outside for some air and a smoke. He was heading for a small store for some provisions. He and his brother stayed out of sight during the day to avoid suspicion. They had been given the name of the YMCA by the Captain of the ship. Now that they arrived in Canada, their plan was simple enough: to try and find some way to get the information they carried to the authorities, but they had no idea who they would be or where to find them. They had discussed the problem earlier that day and decided they would go to the local newspaper and tell their story.

But something went wrong.

Gregori did not know that the NKVD's reach extended this far. Someone in the port city was working for them. How they managed to discover where they were did not matter now. The only thing that mattered to him was it had cost his brother's life. Now here he was, hiding under the protection of the church.

* * *

Not long after he arrived in Halifax, Petrov sought out someone in the criminal underground he could use as a local resource. His name was Martin Wallace. He had his hands in a number of illegal activities: extortion, bootlegging, loan sharking, pimping. To Petrov, he was a worm, a parasite, but he was also someone whose only allegiance, loyalty, was to money and could be easily bought. Petrov had no scruples about dealing with such a person since many of his activities were not unlike those he learned and used himself as a NVKD agent.

Wallace soon proved his worth by putting a number of shady men, and women, to work for him; the men as muscle when needed and the women to get information from certain people using their sex.

He received new coded instructions from his handler in Ottawa to deal with two brothers arriving on the SS Hudson, an eight-thousand-ton tramp steamer that sailed from Arkhangelsk twelve days earlier as part of a return convoy. Its sailing orders included a stop at the port of Halifax to refuel at the refinery there.

According to the report, the captain of this ship was sympathetic to the White Russians cause and worked by helping them get people the NKVD wanted out of Russia. As was the case now. On board were two brothers named, Gregori and Ivan Greshenko, who were charged for crimes against the State and being White Russians. In reality, the coded message said that these brothers had information harmful to the State and must not be allowed to spread it to the Allies. He knew what that meant: he was being ordered to find and assassinate them.

The day the ship arrived he made his way over to the oil refinery on the Dartmouth side of the harbour. He boarded the ship and was taken to the captain's cabin. He informed him that he was from the Embassy and that he was here to arrest two Russians that boarded his ship before sailing.

"There are no Russians on board this ship," the captain said calmly.

"We know that two brothers were placed on board..." Petrov started to say.

"Listen, buster. You don't come on board my ship accusin' me of anythin', got it? I don't give a shit what you've been told, see. You got no authority here, so I'll be tellin' ya ta get off my ship. Now. Or do I call fer the cops?"

The captain sat behind his desk with his hands folded across his slightly large belly, staring at the big Russian.

"This will not go well for you," Petrov said in a threatening tone of voice. "There will be a formal protest."

"JOHNSON," the captain yelled without looking away from him.

A moment later a young man stood in the door. He wore a black woolen jacket with a single gold band around the wrist of each sleeve.

"Sir?" he said, looking from one man to the other.

"Get the bos'n an' a coupla men an' see this man off the ship."

"You will regret this," Petrov said, not hiding his anger. He clearly was not accustomed to dealing with someone who had no fear of him.

"Don't take any guff offa him, jus' see he gets off."

"Aye sir."

Petrov fumed but controlled his anger. He turned on his heels and stormed out of the cabin, pushing the young officer aside. He would make a report to his handler about the incident, making sure that the name of the ship and Captain were dispatched to NKVD headquarters. If the ship showed up in Russia again, he thought. A trace of a smile showed on his face as reached the waiting car that brought him over to the refinery from Halifax.   He climbed in the back of the car.

"Go," he ordered.

"No luck, eh?" the driver said as he shifted the vehicle in gear and headed away.

"Take me to Wallace," was all he said by way of an answer.

He would have to do it the hard way, he thought. Upon his return to Halifax, he called Wallace and ordered him to put his people on the street and find the brothers.

As luck would have it, it was one of his men that found them a day later. He did not know how they found the YMCA and did not care. The only thing Petrov was concerned about was the fact that they would be extremely hard to reach while staying there...too many people.

Chapter Five

The call from Morrison came in at ten-thirty.

"I heard Pete was in asking about a reported killing," he said, without any preamble, as was his manner. "It happens that I just received notice from Kendricks that the body of an unidentified man was found on the rocks down around Purcell's Cove opposite Point Pleasant Park. Looks like it had been in the water for a couple of days."

Kendricks was one of the older detectives in the squad.

"He say how was he killed?" I asked.

"Throat cut. Pretty bad, he says. The cut damn near took the poor bastard's head off."

"I take it there were no papers or anythin'?"

"Correct."

"I think I might have an idea who he was."

Go on."

"Looks like there were two men, brothers, Russians, who escaped from Russia on a ship that was here recently. They were being sought after by the Soviet secret police, the NKVD. Apparently, they have some information the Russians don't want let out. Anyway, people in Ottawa seem to think that this NKVD group has sent an agent or agents here."

"To find these brothers?"

"Partly, accordin' to Michael, the Russians have started spyin' on the Allies for any military secrets. He thinks that's the main reason they're here. The brothers must've been somethin' else."

"I see. Got a name?"

"Greshenko. Ivan Greshenko. The other brother's name is Gregori."

"I don't suppose you know where this one is?"

"He's at St. Mary's. He's requested sanctuary from the church."

"Hell's teeth," Morrison swore, which surprised me since he almost never swore. "This is turning into something we should not be involved in."

"I agree," I said, "but Michael and Phil believe we are the best to deal with this agent."

"I am happy Naval Intelligence thinks so highly of us, but this is their mess. We are not set up or equipped to deal something so politically explosive. I'll have to brief the mayor on this. Also, it seems to me that these two incidents are about to overlap. That being the case, I'm going to recommend that you and Pete continue your investigations for Parks back here so you can take over this dead man business."

"Yes sir. Should I let Michael know?"

"Not yet. Wait until I talk with the mayor. I'll call him at that time."

"Yes sir," I said just before I heard the line go dead. That was Morrison for you.

I hung up and turned back to my notes.

"Whazzup?" Pete asked, looking up from his notebook.

"Don't say anythin', but it looks like we may be headin' back to the station. Seems a dead man's body washed up jus' outside the harbour mouth down by Purcell's Cove. Looks like it could be the missing brother."

"Yeah, so?"

"So that means that case overlaps with what we're lookin' into an' Morrison wants us on it. He's talkin' to the mayor now to make it official."

"Works for me," my friend said. "I don't really like it down here...too many uniforms."

Ten minutes later Michael and Phil came into the room.

"I know," I said as Phil closed the door and Michael stepped up to the table.

"Thought you might when I heard your boss called."

"Sorry 'bout that, but I don't see any problem here since it's a good bet this dead man is the missin' Greshenko brother which means he was likely killed by the NKVD agent, or someone he hired locally. In either case, I think we can do a better job workin' from our own digs."

"We agree," Phil said, taking a chair. I looked from him to Michael who nodded. "The resources here will still be available to you as you need them, and we'll keep you up to date on any relevant information as it comes through."

"Great," I said, "and I'll check in with you daily as well to let you know what we get."

I turned and looked at Michael.

"There's only one matter I need you to clarify for me."

"Let me guess: jurisdiction, yes?" he said with a wry smile.

"Right. We're goin' to be investigatin' a murder now, even if that murder is connected to your issue. The usual governin' legal rules we work by are out the window on this, so what happens if we find your man and he's the one responsible for the killin'?

Do we arrest him, or do you? And if you take him, what about the murder charge?"

"It is a political quagmire to be sure," Michael said. "This man is first a representative of an Ally as well as being an official in that Ally's government. There will be diplomatic issues."

"Screw diplomatic issues," Pete said in his usual blunt way. He had no patience with political machinations. "The bastard murdered someone. Our laws say he's gotta pay for that."

"It isn't that simple," Phil said with a note of sympathy in his voice.

"It is for me."

"Well, we'll deal with all that if and when we lay our hands on this fella an' the evidence needed to bring him to justice," I said, looking at Pete.

"Meanwhile," Michael put in, "I will get in touch with Ottawa. This business now involves civilian authority and that is definitely outside our responsibility here."

There was a brief pause in the conversation then Michael and Phil stood up.

"Just leave the files there on the table," Michael said. "You can take any notes that bear directly on your investigation but not the files marked confidential or secret. They never leave the building. I would appreciate copies of those notes for our records once this matter is resolved, agreed?"

"Understood," I said, standing up.

We put together everything we could take, which was not a lot, and stuffed it into a large brown envelope. I made arrangements with Phil to get one of ratings to drive us back to the station.

When we arrived back at our usual desks, I spotted Kendricks sitting at his desk. I poured a coffee and went over, pulling a nearby chair close.

"Got a coupla minutes?" I asked, sitting down.

"Sure," Kendricks said, looking up from an open file. "Let me guess; this body we found, right?"

George Kendricks was a seasoned detective in the department with six years' experience under his belt. He was ten years younger than me and, like me, has been a career cop. He was married with five kids which he adored, sharing anecdotes about them or their school grades every chance he got. I learned, more by accident, he was also a member of the KoC, the Knights of Columbus, the church's fraternal organization, something akin to the Free Masons.

He was a good detective: clever, quick to pick up on the small details. I worked on a couple cases with him over the years.

"Yeah," I said. "The boss wants me an' Pete to..."

"I got the word already," he said, cutting me off but didn't sound to put out. "Glad to pass it off. I got a lot on my plate an' I haven't committed too much time to the case yet."

"Thanks. So whaddya got so far?"

He pulled a file from the small stack piled on the left side of his desk and passed it to me. It was pretty light.

"As you see, not much. We got a call that a body was found on the beach jus' before ya get to Purcell's Cove. Jack an' me were the duty officers, so went down to check it out." Jack Rawlins was his partner. "So far all we got is a man looks to be in his late twenties, early thirties. Approximately five ten, eleven. One forty, maybe sixty. It was hard to say."

"I don't see the report from the morgue," I said, flipping through the several pages in the file.

"Not in yet. S'pose to be here today or tomorrow."

"What about papers, I.D.?"

"Nothing. All he had on his body was a pack of smokes, a Zippo lighter, a wallet with twelve dollars in it. Didn't even wear a watch."

"So, we can rule out a robbery."

"Yeah, that what's we figured to."

"Who found the body?"

"Name's in there." He nodded toward the file. "One of the locals. Out walkin' his dog."

"For what it's worth, looks like this poor bastard might've been a Russian an' connected to what Pete an' me are workin' on for Naval Intelligence."

"No kiddin'? Well, good luck with it."

"Thanks, I'll take this if that's okay?"

"All yours."

I stood up with the file and my coffee in hand and returned to my desk. I called Pete over.

"I want you to head out an' go talk with the fella that found the body. The information on where he lives is in here," I said, passing him Kendricks' file. "I'm gonna head up to the morgue an' have talk with the M.E. then drop down an' see Michael. I gotta a coupla questions need answers. We'll meet back here later. You can drop me off at the hospital."

"Okay," he said. "This looks like it gonna be a bad one, doesn't it?"

"No more than any other murder investigation," I said," grabbing my hat and coat.

"I'm not so sure. Somethin' jus' don't feel right about it."

"Yeah, well, we'll see as we go. You ready?"

"Yeah."

My meeting at the hospital did not add much to what we already knew. The cause of death was straightforward: death by strangulation. Weapon: some sort of strong cord or wire. Notable features: attack was extremely brutal and suggests that the murderer was strong and most likely a man at least six foot tall. The M.E. added that he estimated the body was in the water between twenty-four and thirty-six hours. One more interesting item about the victim:

the man had definite East European features.

The M.E. also wrote, the pressure applied by the murderer was sufficient to cut into skin, tissue, and muscle, adding that if only a bit more pressure was applied, he would have potentially decapitated the head.

Christ, I thought, when I finished the report, this man must be a monster.

Before leaving the hospital, I called ahead to make sure Michael was in. I decided to walk down to the headquarters building, taking the opportunity to process the information I had so far. It was a short walk and I arrived there fifteen minutes later.

When I reached Michael's office, the young WAVE Sub-lieutenant that served as his secretary waved me on through with a warm smile.

"Ah, Robie," Michael said from behind his desk. "Take a pew. What news?"

"I jus' got hold of the open case file by the detective who was first on the scene," I said. "Not much in it yet except the usual stuff: initial report, name of witnesses an' so on. Pete's down in Purcell's Cove interviewin' the man who found the body."

"But you are still going on the assumption that this dead man is one of the Russian brothers?" he asked.

"Until evidence proves the contrary, yeah. I jus' come down from the hospital where I talked to the M.E." I gave him the dime novel version of what I learned.

"He also said that the victim had the features you'd usually find in people from Eastern Europe. Russia is in that area."

"True. Any ideas why or how this ties in with this possible agent?"

"If I read what the other brother told me right, and what you an' Phil said, then back over there in Russia, this NKVD bunch operates like secret police with some wide-reachin' powers. Also, from what the brother told me, Stalin seems to be piling up quite a stack of bodies, mostly his own people. That's why they fled; to try an' get the information out to rest of the world."

"That appears to be supported by reports coming out of Russia according to MI5."

"Then why in hell are we still supportin' the bastard?"

"We still need Russia to fight the Germans. It may look like they are on the run but by all accounts, they are still seen as a strong army. If the Russians pull out the Western Front could be serious jeopardy."

"Jesus," I said. "What a way to fight a war."

"No argument from me," he said, sharing my feeling.

"Happily, that's not my concern. Findin' this guy is. To that point, it would help me if you can get me any information on the NKVD."

"What sort of information specifically?"

"I'm not sure but it'd help if I had some idea of how they operate."

"Hmm. I am not sure what I can get for you, but I will make some calls. Anything else?"

"Yeah. It'd also help if I knew more 'bout the political side of this business. Phil said there might be some complications from that side once we find this man. I've learned the hard way jus' how messed up a case can get when politicians stick their oar in."

"I cannot promise much but again, I'll see what I can do."

"Thanks."

"I can tell you this much," he said, leaning forward with his arms on the desk, "I have been told that the NKVD have a reputation for using extremely brutal tactics including torture and murder. They are also the administers of the Russian penal system called gulags, or labour camps. Rumours are that being sent there is akin to death sentence. So, my friend, if only a part of the stories are true I would ask that you and Pete step very carefully with this man."

"You can count on that," I said. "Thanks for sharin' that with me and for anythin' else you get. I'll check again tomorrow or if we get anythin' before then."

"Anytime, my friend. Be careful."

I decided to head back to the station and see if Pete was back with anything useful. I stepped outside just in time to catch the northbound tram. It was crammed full as usual, and I had to stand the whole ride.

When I reached the squad room, I saw that Pete was not back yet, so I got a coffee and went over the notes and information Michael Parks just gave me.

Twenty minutes later Pete stepped into the room. He hung up his overcoat and then came and sat beside my desk, taking out his notebook.

"How'd you make out?" I asked.

"It took a while to find the man who reported findin' the body," he said. "His name is John Purcell. Lived in the Cove all his life apparently. Up to a coupla years ago he worked as a fisherman. More or less called it quits after his wife died but stayed on since his family lives around the area. He seems to like goin' for a lotta walks with his dog."

"That's more than was in the file."

"He's got a coupla chatty neighbours."

"Go on."

"When I finally managed to speak with him, he didn't have a whole lot more to say than what he told Kendricks. He was out walking his dog when he saw a body lying on the rocks. He figured it got washed up as the tide went out. Said the first thing he did was to go an' see if it was someone from the cove. When he saw it wasn't he went an' called it in," he said, closing his notebook.

"That it?"

"Yeah. How'd you make out at the hospital?"

"The cause of death was strangulation. Apparently by someone strong enough to almost take the poor bastard's head off. Doc figures he was in the water no more than thirty-six hours and he thinks he was East European."

"That it? Ain't much," Pete said.

I shrugged.

"Granted, we haven't had a case with so little to go on. I stopped off and had a talk with Parks. This business with this Soviet agent an' now this dead man who looks like he might be Russian, raises a lotta questions. An' it doesn't help that it comes with a shit load of political headaches."

"No kiddin'," he said. "So, what'd he say? Anythin' useful?"

"Not much. One thing is clear from what he knows, we gotta be especially careful. This agent works for an agency with a reputation for usin' extremely brutal tactics an' has no compunction 'bout murderin' anyone. So, until this case is done, we always go armed an' ready to use deadly force."

"Jesus."

"I think our next steps will be to hit the streets an' roust up our snitches, see if there's any word out there 'bout this guy. If he's here, then I'm guessin' he's hooked up with some lowlife to help him. In the meantime, I gonna upstairs to see the boss an' fill him in."

"Okay." Pete stood up and headed for his desk and I headed for the stairs.

* * *

Three men sat around a wooden table in a kitchen drinking beer. One of them, a man named Charlie Roode, looked shaken, his eyes staring at the dark green quart bottle in front of him.

"You say you saw him kill this bloke?" Henry Wallace asked.

Wallace was the leader of a small gang operating in the city. He had about a dozen men on his payroll, half of them were cab drivers he used to courier his booze and women to customers. He dealt mostly in bootlegging, pimping, loan sharking and fencing stolen goods. Originally from Canso down by Cape Breton, he arrived in Halifax at the outbreak of the war. He already had a reputation and was known to the local criminal fraternity.

Roode slowly raised his eyes to look at his boss and nodded.

"I ain't never gonna fergit it," he said, his voice cracking a little. "Da look on that poor sod's face when he pulled the wire tight. Then the blood...Jesus, I taut his 'ead was gonna come off."

"Okay, then what?"

"He tole me ta git da car an' den we stuff the body inta da boot. We drive down ta Melville Cove an' dump it inta da water. He sez it'll go out wit da tide. Den I take 'im back inta town."

"Christ Almighty," the third man said. His name was Joe Sampson. "What we get ourselves inta, Hank? This fella sounds like a cold-hearted sonofabitch. We ain't ever been involved in killin'."

"Yeah, I know," Wallace said. "It's too late now. We're in it."

"So whadda we gonna do?" he asked.

Roode went back to staring at his beer.

"Bide our time so's I can work somethin' out."

"Whadda we do if the police get wind of any a this? I don't know 'bout you, but I ain't keen on havin' to watch over my shoulder for Robichaud or his pit bull, Duncan."

"We don't hafta worry 'bout that," Wallace said. "He's got no way 'a knowin' we're involved. Only da three of us here know we're in it. As long as we keep our mouths shut, we oughta be in the clear."

"Well, I ain't gonna tell anyone," Sampson said, picking up his bottle and taking a swallow.

Wallace looked to Roode who raised his eyes to meet his.

"Ya got nothin' ta worry 'bout from me," he said. "I ain't never gonna talk 'bout that. All I wanna do is wipe it outta my head."

"That's that then," Wallace said. "We keep business as usual, see. An' I'll see what I can do to get us clear 'a this prick."

Chapter Six

I made my way through a half dozen taverns and bootleggers before I caught up with one of my best snitches: Gerry Taylor.

Taylor was a local street hustler and sometime cab driver. He was born here to a fairly well-to-do family but somewhere along the way to adulthood he strayed into a life of petty crime and was subsequently disowned by his family. I'd known him for more than ten years now and he had proved a useful source of information on what was happening in the city. Turns out, he has a sense of right and wrong, at least by his standards.

I caught up with him down near the bottom of Barrington Street where it meets Inglis. He was in the basement of a bootlegger's house, sitting with a couple of his cronies enjoying a bottle of beer.

When I managed to catch his eye, I tilted my head slightly, signaling for him to come outside then turned and stepped back outside. He stepped out a few minutes later and, spotting my car, walked over, and got in.

"Hey Robie," he said with a jovial tone of voice. I reckoned he had a couple of beers already.

"Gerry," I said. "How're things?"

"Oh, ya know, the usual shit. What's up?"

"I need a favour."

"Shoot. Always happy ta help the boys in blue."

"First. You hear anythin' 'round town 'bout a Russian lookin' for a connection?"

"A Russian?"

"Yeah. May have come here in the last few weeks or so."

"What sorta connection ya mean?"

"With one 'a da gangs. Maybe lookin' to hire some muscle, ya know, that sorta t'ing."

"Hm, now you mention it, yeah. I seem ta remember hearin' somethin'. A coupla the lads said word's out that Wallace was lookin' for some men."

"Henry Wallace?"

"Is there any other Wallace ya know?"

"They say what kind of work he was hirin' for?" I asked.

"Nope, jus' that he was lookin' for a coupla men," Gerry said. "'Though, I hafta say I was a bit puzzled. I mean, Wallace is small time compared to some I could name. What's goin' on? I mean, here you are askin' if I heard anythin' 'bout some Russian in connection with any of the gangs..."

"Look," I said cutting him off. "Keep your ears an' eyes open an' call me if you pick up anythin', especially 'bout this Russian. Okay?"

"Yeah...yeah, sure thing. By the way, I heard there's this woman, a Frenchie, no offense. Maybe in from Quebec. Anyway, word is she's been stirrin' up some of a locals Frenchmen; spreadin' anti-war crap and such."

"Got a name?"

"Dumont, or somethin' like that."

"Okay, thanks. An' Gerry, be careful. This guy is a killer. Get anythin', call me. Got it?" I said as I passed him a ten-dollar bill. He nodded with a smile, said thanks, and exited the car.

I started the motor and pulled away, heading back to the station. It was an interesting chat with Taylor, especially the part about Henry Wallace putting out a call for a couple men, and the Frenchwoman. I remembered Phil mentioning something about their reports saying the Russian might be traveling with a woman.

I have read in the papers that there was a strong anti-war movement up in Quebec, mostly from the group wanting to separate from the country. I had a hard time trying to understand why. I had some French in my background as well as native Indian but never considered myself any different from anybody else because of it. My only issue had ever been the way the government dealt

95

with the different peoples. I put all that behind me once I left and went to war in nineteen-fourteen. I learned the hard way that when it's on the line, we are all just people; good and bad.

Pete was on his phone when I entered the squad room. I poured a coffee before going to my desk.

"That was Mike Butler," he said when he hung up and came across. Mike Butler was a barman and sometime bouncer at a speakeasy run by a man named, Bert Young. It was a known hangout for many of the city's lowlifes.

He and Pete went way back to when he walked a beat. Butler was a semi-pro fighter with a promising career until one fight he refused to take a dive. When he was jumped outside the Forum by a couple of the mobster's men, Pete just happened to be going by and weighed in to help him. He has been a source of information for Pete ever since.

"What'd he have to say?" I asked.

"When I mentioned the Russian, he said he's heard about him. Seems this Russian is goin' round the boozers askin' questions 'bout some brothers. He's been tellin' anybody who'd listen, he has news from home for them."

"He say if anybody take the bait?"

"No. But the crowd that goes to Young's place aren't dopes. An' it seems that many of them aren't all that partial to Russians;

or maybe jus' to this particular Russian. I asked him if he ever talked to or seen the Russian. He said he saw him one time. He said there was somethin' 'bout him that spooked him."

"Yeah? Like what?"

"He wasn't specific, but he said there was definitely somethin' made you want to cross the street when you saw him comin'. How 'bout you, anythin'?"

"I had a chat with Gerry Taylor. He said he's been hearin' that Wallace put the word out for a coupla men."

Henry Wallace?" Pete said, raising an eyebrow. "I wouldn't a thought he had the moxy for somethin' this big."

"Neither did I," I said. "But it looks like it's possible he's thrown in with the Russian. He does know the city an' has the resources the Russian needs if he is lookin' for the Greshenkos."

"True. You think he'd also be helpin' him get his hands on our secrets?"

"He is a weasel an' would sell his mother if there was enough in it, so, yeah, I reckon he would."

"He have those sort a connections, you know, with the people who have the secrets?"

"Maybe. If they drink, gamble, or have a taste for certain types of women. You know the type, same as me."

"Yeah," he said. "I do. So, what do we do?"

"Let's go have a talk with him."

"Wouldn't that sorta tip our hand? You know, if he is workin' for the Russian, he'd warn him."

"True. But I think it might pay off in our favour if the Russian knows we're onto him. If nothin' else it'd put him on the defensive."

"Yeah an' maybe get someone killed."

We grabbed our coats and headed for the stairs leading up to the parking area.

Henry Wallace owned a wooden two-story house down on Atlantic Street just in from Inglis. When we arrived, I saw several cars parked there: one in the driveway beside the house, the others nearby on the street. There was also a half dozen men in uniform, mostly sailors, milling around the front of the house. Not surprising since he ran a bootlegging operation out of his cellar.

We parked, got out and headed for the front door, pushing past one or two young sailors who eyed us suspiciously.

I did not bother to knock when we reached the door and stepped into the small foyer. There were sounds of men talking and laughing and the occasional clink of glass on glass.

Moving down the hall towards the kitchen in the rear of the house, we found Wallace standing at a cast iron wood burning stove, stirring something in a large metal pot; smelled like a chowder of some kind. He glanced over his shoulder when he heard us come in.

"What da 'ell you want?" he sneered, turning back to the pot.

"We want to have a little chat," I said. "So put the ladle down an' take seat."

I pulled one of wooden chairs out from the table and sat down; Pete stood at the door, hands in his overcoat pockets.

"Screw you. Ya got no right..."

"Look, you can sit down an' do this the easy way, or we'll drag your sorry ass outta here an' do this at the station."

"You're a piece a fuckin' work, ya prick," Wallace snapped, turning to face both of us then, after a moment, reluctantly took a seat across from me. "I'm sittin'. Git on wit it. Yer spoilin' my chowder."

"First, watch your mouth or soup'll be all you be able to eat for a while," Pete said threatcningly. I saw him shift his eyes quickly from me to Pete then back to me.

"Good. I'm here to ask you a coupla questions 'bout a Russian that's in town. Word is you're doin' some work for him." I noted the look of surprise that suddenly came into his eyes.

"Wh...what Russian? I don't know what yer talkin' about," he stammered.

"Forget tryin' to bullshit us. We're onto you an' him. What I want to know is anythin' you know 'bout a Russian who turned up dead a coupla days ago."

"Why would I know anythin' 'bout a dead Russian?" He was regaining his footing. "Ya got nothin' connectin' me wit any killin'."

"Not yet," I said, "but when I do, I'll be down on you like a ton of shit. Got it?"

I stood up and looked own into his face.

"Jus' a quick piece of advice, not that I give a shit what happens to you, but, if we find out you're hooked up with the Russian I'll turn you over to Naval Intelligence. That'd mean you'll be dealt with by the military. So do yourself a favour an' tell your Russian friend, if he's got a brain to pack up an' get out of town. We're on to him an' if stays it won't go well for him. Enjoy the chowder. Smells good."

As we walked back down the hall, I heard him mutter, "Fuck you."

Back in the car Pete whistled then said, "Jesus, I knew you were goin' to tip our hand but..."

"If you're goin' to send a message then send a clear one," I said, shifting into gear. "But I did learn two things."

"Yeah. What?'

"One. He is workin' with the Russian."

"An' two?"

"He can cook a great chowder." We both broke out in laughter.

Within minutes of us leaving, Wallace was on the phone to Petrov.

"It's me," he said when Petrov answered.

"What do you want? Did I not tell you no call?"

"I had ta. Da cops were jus' here. They know all 'bout ya."

"What?"

"Da cops, dey know all 'bout ya an' me."

"What they say? What they know?" Petrov demanded.

"They didn't say."

"Then how they know?"

"I don't know, but they tole me they know 'bout a Russian an' some other Russian that was killed. Jesus, what da 'ell we gonna do?" Wallace said.

"Stay calm. Let me think." There was a long pause, then, "What else they say?"

"Da cop, Robichaud, he sez to tell ya da jig is up an' fer ya to git out of town."

"What is 'jig'?

"Ya know, da business, da shit we's inta."

"I see. Who is this, Robichaud?"

"He's the head of da detectives on da police force. A real prick."

"He can be bought?"

"Not him, no sir. Straight arrow."

"Hmmm. Anyway to get at him?"

"Whaddya talkin' 'bout, git at 'im?"

"Woman? Family?"

"Hey, I ain't gittin' involved wit goin' after him or his family, see."

"You will do as you are told," Petrov said, coldly. "Or else we have problem, understand?"

"Yeah, I unnerstan," Wallace said nervously.

"Good. Now you get me information on this, er, cop, da?"

"Like what?"

"Where he lives. His family."

Christ almighty, Wallace thought. This had become more than just a chance to score a good payday. The more he realized the implications of what the Russian planned to do, the more he felt the rope tighten around his throat.

He had to find a way to get out from under and not pay too high a price in doing so.

"Okay," he said then the line went dead.

Joe Sampson came into the room just as he was hanging up the phone.

"Jesus, boss," he said. "You okay? You look like..."

"Huh? Yeah...yeah, I'm okay. That was da Russian."

"What'd he want dis time?" he asked, sitting down on one of the deep cushioned chairs in the front room.

"He's plannin' on goin' for Robichaud; maybe his family too."

"Shit. That mean he wants us to...ya know?"

Wallace shrugged and shook his head.

"Don't know. All he wants is information on Robichaud for now."

"You ain't seriously plannin' on killin' a cop, are ya?"

"You t'ink I'm crazy," Wallace snapped. "Christ, if I'm gonna kill anybody it'd be the fuckin' Russian."

"No shit," Sampson said.

"Who do we know we kin git to do da job?"

"You're serious?"

"Don't see any other way, do you?"

"Guess not. Only one I know who'd be crazy enough to take the job is Kelly Johns."

Kelly Johns was a native Indian from down Yarmouth way. He was in his fifties and known around the city as a local 'character' who will do anything for a drink. Some said, he became addicted to whisky early on in his life eventually causing some brain damage, or so it was believed by some doctors who had occasion to examine him after an arrest. He was generally harmless when sober and would even take a legit job once in a while. But when he was on the bottle; well, that was another story.

A few of the loan sharks in town would use him at times when they needed to resort to rough stuff to collect on late payers. Rumour has that at least two deaths could be laid at Johns feet. The police who arrested him often found a large hunting knife strapped to his forearm that he reportedly knew how to use.

"Get in touch with 'im."

"Ya sure 'bout dis?" Sampson asked. He wasn't looking forward to dealing with the

Indian. "Ya know he's not right in da 'ead, right?"

"Jus' bring 'im 'ere," Wallace ordered.

Chapter Seven

The next day dawned overcast with a raw damp northeasterly wind coming down off the Basin; the kind of wind that cut through everything you wore and chilled the very bones. By the time I arrived at the station, my mood was as cold as the day outside.

I managed to get a seat on the tram for a change. Things were changing these days as most people began to let themselves believe the war was nearing an end. The thing I noticed most was the lack of urgency that had prevailed over the city for the last four years. Mind, there still was a large military presence and the waterfront buzzed with a steady stream of ships, now mostly, cargo ships loading materials for Europe. There were a lot less reports of losses to U-boats in the papers lately.

I got off the tram at the corner of Duke Street and dashed between the flow of cars and trucks to the City Hall Building where the police operated from the basement.

The reception area was as busy as always, mostly townspeople with a wide range of complaints as well as a number of uniformed men, some still drunk from a night of cavorting. The room felt hot and not just from the heat of so many bodies.

"Robie," someone yelled over the mob of people in the cramped area around the duty officer's desk.

It was Bill Kennedy, the duty Sergeant. He was holding up a piece of paper and waving at me. I muscled my way past several disgruntled civilians vying for Kennedy's attention. There were also several uniformed cops and sailors there; the sailors looked the worse for wear.

"Yeah?" I said when I reached his post.

"This came in twenty minutes ago," he said, passing the piece of paper to me. "Sez to call as soon as ya got in. Sez it's important."

"Who?"

"Yer Mountie friend, Mulroney."

"Okay. Thanks."

I took the slip of paper and made my way to the door leading to the squad room. My spot was immediately taken by some man with a bushy mustache.

After settling in at my desk with a fresh mug of coffee, I dropped my newspaper and reached for the phone.

"You called?" I said once I reached Phil.

"Yeah," he said. "Something's come in you need to see."

"When?"

"As soon as you can spare the time."

"Alright." I looked up at the wall clock: six-forty-five. "I be there in half an hour."

"Thanks. See you then."

I hung up and picked up my coffee, taking a swig, enjoying the heat as it eased down my throat. I always enjoyed that first coffee of the day and the feeling of the rich caffeine as it entered my system. I started to write a note for Pete, letting him know where I was at if he needed me.

I found Phil in his office. Like me, he preferred to come in earlier before the business of the day came rushing in. He looked up from an open dossier on his desk when I entered the office.

"Mornin'," I said, taking a chair in front of the desk. "You look like crap."

"Thanks," he said with a smile. "Nice of you to say."

"Sorry. Got a bit of a crank on. What's up?"

"This came in overnight." He passed the dossier across to me.

"Looks like this Russian has made a connection with someone, or maybe more than one, working in sensitive areas at the shipyard, possibly even the dockyard. One of the managers thinks some documents have gone missing and there are indications that certain papers have been misfiled."

I looked up from the document and asked, "How sure is he someone has been tampering with the files?"

"Pretty sure. He's the mainly responsible for the security of the file room."

"Sounds like this is something for your people," I said, passing the dossier back to him.

"It is," he said, taking the dossier. "I put a man on it; Wilkins, you remember him?"

"Yeah. Good man as I recall."

"He is. He's going to see the manager, but he needs a bit of help which I can't give him right now. So, I'd like you to go with him."

"Sure, why not."

"Thanks. How is your investigation going by the way?"

"Looks like our guy has connected with a local villain. A small-time operator name of Henry Wallace. Runs booze, prostitutes, and loan sharkin'. To be honest with you, I don't see him havin' the resources the Russian needs. I plan to lean on him to give the Russian over."

"I knew we did the right thing bringing you two in...as usual."

"When do you want me an' Wilkins to head down?"

"He's getting ready as we speak. You'll find him in his office down the hall. He's expecting you, and Robie, thanks again."

"No problem."

Carl Wilkins was one of the Mounties bright young officers: a university graduate with a proven instinct for solving crimes. At twenty-seven, he was well on his way up the ladder to Inspector. Since our last meeting he had earned his stripes and was now a corporal.

I knocked on his door as I opened it.

"Detective," he said with a war, friendly smile. "Good to see you again."

"You too," I said. "And it's Robie."

"Thanks."

"I see congratulations are in order." I nodded towards his uniform jacket.

"Huh? Oh, yes, thanks."

"So? Ready?"

"Yes sir, uh, Robie."

"How do you want handle this when we get there?"

"What do you mean?"

"This is your bailiwick. I'm along to help."

"Right. We're going to meet with a Mr. Luc Allard. He's actually employed by Davie Shipyards in Quebec but was sent here as part of a deal. His main responsibility is to oversee certain parts of the shipyard's operations, including the security of sensitive files and documents."

"Okay, let's go. My car or yours?"

"Yours'll do."

We headed down the hall and out of the building.

The drive down to the shipyard was relatively quick, traffic was surprisingly light for the time of day. I turned off Barrington Street at the north end of the dockyard then left and down to the security gate. I could see the slips were busy with ships in for repairs.

Even though Wilkins was dressed in his uniform he still showed his ID card, and I showed the guard my badge.

"We're expected," Wilkins said. "Mr. Luc Allard."

The guard wrote down our names and who we were seeing as well as the time then waved us through.

"That it for security?" I asked. This was my first time in the facility since the outbreak of the war.

"Pretty much," Wilkins said. "They have roving patrols of MPs and sometimes the navy has their own people when any of their ships are being worked on. It tough to regulate the place with so many workers working here on a twenty-four-hour basis."

He pointed to a large brick building.

"That's the administration Building."

I pulled into a vacant spot and shut the motor off. We got out and walked to the entrance.

Inside the reception area we were greeted by two SP sailors in full battle dress, including the helmet, sometimes called the 'soup bowl'. They each wore a pistol on their webbing, probably the standard British

Webley .38 and carried a Lanchester MK 1 sub-machine gun, both standard issue in the navy.

Once our IDs were confirmed, Wilkins led the way upstairs. Allard's office was on the third floor. I couldn't help noticing how busy the place was with men and women filling the hall and the sounds of chatter and typing coming from the rooms we passed.

"In here," Wilkins said as he opened a glass paneled door marked simply with the number 312 printed in black on it.

"Ah," the man sitting behind a grey metal desk said as he stood up. "Morning. Good to see you again Constable, er, Corporal. Congratulations."

He reached his hand across the desk to Wilikns while keeping his eyes on me.

"Thanks," Wilkins said, accepting his hand. "This here is Detective Robichaud. IIe's with thc city police but works with us sometimes. His local knowledge has proven invaluable."

"G'day," I said as he offered his hand to me.

"Bon jour. Or would you be more comfortable in English?"

"English'll do jus' fine, thanks."

"Please." He waved us to take a seat. We pulled a couple of wooden chairs over and sat down.

"So. You called to say you suspect something is going on?" Wilkins said, getting right to the business at hand.

"Yes. I have noticed lately that several rather sensitive documents have gone missing or have been misfiled."

"What sort of documents are we talkin' about?" I asked.

He gave me a funny look then turned his gaze to Wilkins."

"It's okay," Wilkins said. "Robie has been cleared to Top Secret."

"Ah. All the documents were from the technology files; sonar, radar, weapons systems, that sort of thing."

"How long has this been going on?"

"About a month, maybe two. I picked up on the discrepancies then."

Wilkins and I exchanged glances.

"This means something?" Allard asked.

"We suspect there is a Soviet agent here to try and obtain this type of information," Wilkins said.

"But aren't they our allies? My God, we just finished a minor repair on a small Russian freighter. Storm damage on the last crossing."

"When you called, you said something about possible suspects?" Wilkins went on.

"As you know, when I came here to set up the security system, the first thing I did was to institute a record keeping procedure to control access and where the documents were at all times. Two days ago, I looked through the sign in and out ledgers after I was told that one of the technicians could not find a set of schematics for a weapon

112

system component. It was then that noticed a name that did not belong."

"Not belong?" I asked. "What do you mean by that?"

"It was not a name of any technician I was aware of."

I nodded.

"When I contacted personnel and asked if there was any record of anyone named Lawrence Mitchell on the payroll, I was told there was a man by that name working in the electrical shop down in the dockyard as an electrician."

"Do people in that shop have clearance to the file room?" Wilkins asked.

"No. Only managers and cleared technicians have access."

"Is it possible to get hold 'a this guy's personnel file?" I asked.

Allard opened a desk drawer, and pulled out a manila folder, and passed it over to me.

"I assumed you would want it."

"Thanks." I opened the folder. There were several pages inside; the usual stuff an employee's file would contain. "We'll need to take this with us."

"That will not be a problem."

"What steps have you taken? Did you contact this Mitchell?" Wilkins asked.

"No. I thought it best to wait until I spoke with your office first. Besides, the shipyard is not set up to take any police action only to prevent something like this from happening. Steps have been taken to ensure there is a tighter control."

"For the time being, it might be useful to us if you don't implement any changes until we pick this guy up," I said this to Wilkins who nodded his agreement.

"Fine," Allard said.

"Thank you," Wilkins said. "Keep me informed if any more discrepancies come to light."

We all stood up and after shaking hands again, we left, returning to the car.

"You think this Mitchell is working for the Russian?"

"Can you think of any other reason he'd be stealing those documents?" I asked as he pulled out of the parking slot and headed for the gate.

"No, not really. Anything useful in his employment file?"

"Not much. Address. Work history. Qualifications. The usual. I am curious 'bout one thing?"

"What's that?"

"There's no mention 'bout his security status. I would've thought anyone workin' in a place like the shipyard or dockyard would've had at least a basic background check?"

"I agree," he said, turning south onto Barrington. "Problem is there's just too many people working in those areas and the turnover rate is high. There is a basic check, mostly through contacts with previous employers. The only ones that undergo a more thorough check are the ones who work in sensitive areas."

"Might be somethin' needs updatin' maybe. Do me a favour an' drop me at the station."

"Sure thing. You going to hang onto that folder?'

"For a day or two, if that's okay. I wanna take a good look at this fella. I'll make sure it's safe an' turn it over to you when I'm done."

"No problem."

Back at the station, I got a mug of coffee and went to my desk to read the folder. I scanned the relevant information:

Lawrence (Larry) Mitchell.
Age: 28
Education: Public   school matriculated grade 12
2 years Industrial school – field: electrician, electronics, passed honours
4 year apprenticeship completed at Moir's Chocolate 1 year and Imperoyal 3 years
Known Associates:
Linda Cosgrove, casual friend, employed at Eaton's, sales clerk
William Murray, casual friend, employed in dockyard carpenter in woodworking shop
Jack Markham, employed at shipyard – electronics technician

*Corey Sutherland, casual friend,
employed – auto mechanic Willow Park
service depot
Current address: 16 Maynard Street
Security check: Passed*

A quick scan of the rest of the file provided nothing of interest. It was mostly his work history and references and copies of his certifications. One thing was evident, this fella would certainly know what to look for in the files. There was still one more place to check.

I reached for my phone and dialed the three digits for the records office.

"Records," a woman said in a cheery voice.

"Carol," I said, "it's Robie."

"Robie. My God, it's been a while since you called me."

"Yeah, it has. Do me a favour an' see if we have anythin' on record for Lawrence Mitchell. Last known address 16 Maynard Street an' get back to me."

"Mitchell. Right away. Anything else?"

"Yeah, now that you ask. Send me what we got on Henry Wallace."

"Okay. I recognize him. I'll have it sent down in an hour."

"Thanks,"

"By the way," she said before I hung up. "How are Louise and the kids?"

"Everybody's doin' great. Lou is, you know, Lou. The kids, well what can I say.

116

They're at that age an' all this war stuff is excitin'."

I heard her chuckle. She and my wife went to elementary school together.

"Yeah, I hear you. Mine aren't any better. Give her my regards."

"Will do." I hung up.

Forty minutes later a uniformed cop stepped into the squad room and deposited a thick file on my desk: it was the Wallace file.

"Carol said to tell ya there's nothin' on file for Mitchell," he said.

"Okay, thanks." He turned heel and left.

I spent the next half hour going through Wallace's file. Most of it was not new to me since a lot of the information there was supplied by either Pete or me.

Pete arrived back an hour later.

"Anythin' new?" I asked.

"Not a lot," he said. "I poked 'round at some of the usual places. Seems the Russian is playin' it close to his chest. Doesn't go to any of the usual spots."

"I might've lucked onto something."

I filled him in on my visit to the shipyard and passed the Mitchell folder to him to look at.

"You think this Mitchell might be gettin' information out for the Russian?" he asked when I finished.

"It's a possibility," I said with a shrug. "He'd know what to take."

"Don't they have security down there to protect this information?"

"Yeah, but it doesn't look to be as tight as it could be. It's mostly access by signin' in an' out. That's how we found the name."

"So, what now? We go talk with this guy?"

"Not yet," I said. "If he is the connection then I want keep him on the line, see if he's workin' on his own. However, I think I'll have a talk with Phil an' see if he can spring a coupla his lads for a few days an' set up surveillance on Mitchell."

"Not our people?" Pete asked.

"I think our guys might go unseen by Mitchell but not a trained Russian agent. Phil's people might, or at least he can maybe bring some people in with better skill."

"Never thought 'a that. By the way. What're we doin' 'bout the other brother?"

"Nothin'. As far as I know, Michael is takin' care of that," I said. "But I better check in with him an' see where he's at on it."

"What do you want me to do now?"

"Until I get some set up with Phil, you round up a few of our boys an' get them onto Mitchell. You know who best to use."

"When do we start?"

"Right away. Go up an' clear it with the boss. I'm off to Naval Headquarters. I'll check back here before I head home."

"Okay."

"Hey Robie. Gotta sec?" Jack Rawlins called out. He was another detective and partnered with Kendricks.

"What's up?" I said, walking over to his desk.

"I was talkin' with one a my squealers last night. He said sumthin' might be useful to yer investigation."

"Yeah?"

"Seems a mate of his, fella named Roode, ya know him. A flunky workin' for Wallace. I heard ya tellin' Pete that Wallace might be involved wit this dead Russian case. Anyway, he tells me that Roode's been on a tear the last coupla nights. Sez he's pretty rattled 'bout sumthin'. Thought ya might wanna look into it."

"Thanks Jack, I will. Hear anythn' else let me or Pete know, okay?"

"No sweat."

"By the way, you know where I find Roode?'

"Hangs out at Clark's place over on Garrish."

"I know the place," I said, "an' thanks again."

I headed for the stairs and the parking lot up in the Grand Parade Grounds.

* * *

Nikolai Petrov lay in his bed smoking a cigarette, staring up at the single shaded light hanging from a twisted cord in the

119

ceiling. He had one arm tucked under the pillow, the other lay across his naked chest; the cigarette wedged between two fingers over an ashtray sitting on top of the sheet covering his lower body.

He was going through all that he had achieved of his mission since arriving in this city. He had secured two reliable sources of information, good information which he was sending back to his controller in Ottawa. He managed to eliminate one of the brothers as ordered and now only had to find the other one. Wallace's people still had no luck in locating him or picking up any word on the street about him. This frustrated him. The brother was an inconvenience he wanted to be rid of and the sooner the better.

But now he had a new problem to contend with – this policeman: Detective John Robichaud.

If the information Wallace passed on was correct, then this policeman might know about his presence and that could also mean his mission. Wallace also found out that Robichaud has been connected to the local branch of Naval Intelligence. That posed a greater problem and risk, he realized as he absentmindedly took a drag on his cigarette, blowing a cloud of grey smoke up toward the ceiling. He would normally just make the men disappear, either to a gulag or a grave, but he was not home in Russia and such actions would be his undoing in this country. He would have to move carefully from now on. He would have to be less direct, be more adroit. Fortunately, his training included the use of more subtle techniques: finding and attacking the most vulnerable areas of his target; in this case, his family.

However, he would soon learn at great cost that fear and intimidation would not work here. But for the moment, his thoughts were interrupted by the slow stirring of the young woman lying next to him as she rolled to face him, slipping her warm hand down over his stomach.

Chapter Eight

I arrived at Naval Headquarters and, after clearing the security check, headed upstairs. I was told Phil and Michael were down in the cafeteria located in the basement. They were sitting at a table away from the other people in the room; mostly ratings of both sexes either eating a meal or just on a break.

When Phil spotted me, he waved me over. I nodded and made my way to the refreshment area and poured a mug of tea then went and joined them.

"What brings you in?" Michael asked. "Any news?"

"Not a lot," I said, settling onto the hard wooden chair. "I think we've identified a local villain probably workin' for the Russian."

"So, you are saying that we can say the Russians have placed an agent here?"

"Yeah, looks that way."

"But still no idea where to find him?"

"Not yet, but I'm workin' a few angles might turn somethin". If he's here in the city, we'll find him."

"I know you will," Parks said. "It is the reason I requested you and Pete to help us out. You are so good at what you do."

"You say you found the local contact?" Phil spoke for the first time. "Is it this Wallace you mentioned before?'

"Uh-huh," I said looking at him, nodding.

"And you know this how?"

"Let's jus' say a few little birds..." I left it hanging there, assuming Phil would understand. He did.

"Gotcha."

"What are your next moves?" Michael asked.

"First thing will be to follow up on the information we received. We know the people namcd an' how to shake them up. They're weasels mostly; sell their mothers if it'd bring them a buck or get them out from under. I figure if I put the squeeze on them, I can get one to rollover on the Russian, maybe even Wallace."

"Doesn't that run the risk of exposing our involvement?"

"Can't be helped, not if you want results. Besides, I suspect the Russian already knows we're on to him, at the very least suspects we are."

"Why?" Michael asked. In many ways Michael Parks was a brilliant intelligence man but had no idea of the realities of street level criminals.

"The dead brother," Phil put in.

"Oh."

"Speakin' of which, what's the latest on the other brother?"

"We picked him up," Michael said, "and secured him in the one place where the Russian cannot reach him: on one of her majesty's warships presently in harbour. A man is coming down from Ottawa to interview him. By all indications, the information he is carrying on Stalin's atrocities are, well, let me just say that it will likely have far-reaching consequences."

"Good to hear," I said. "Do you need me to continue workin' with Wilkins?"

"For the moment, yes. I understand from his report you have a name of a man who may be of interest regarding missing documents?"

"That's right," I said. "I was waitin' to hear what action you were goin' to take before doin' anythin'."

"If this man is the leak, then he is likely acting under the Russian's orders so, for the moment, I am quite happy to leave the matter in your capable hands. Wilkins will work with you for the time being as this is still a security matter. Agreed?"

"Okay with me, but remember, my main interest in getting' this bastard is for the murder of Greshenko."

"Our interests are not in conflict, Robie," Michael said. "Ours is to obtain as much information as possible from him, once done he's all yours and the hangman as far as I am concerned. Well, it seems that we have come to the end for now. I must leave you two for other business. Good work as always, Robie."

He stood up and walked off.

"He's lookin' tired," I said, following him with my eyes.

"Who isn't," Phil said.

"That's the truth. Back to Wilkins. You want me to work outta here with him or can he come to the station?"

"Oh, I think the station would be okay. He can report back here at the end of the day."

"Good." I picked up my mug and finished off the last of the tea then stood up. "If you're done with me, I'll head out. Thanks for the tea."

"Yeah, okay," he said. "Thanks for coming down. I'll arrange for Wilkins to head down to the station today."

"See ya," I said with a nod.

Wilkins showed up at the station an hour later, looking eager and serious at the same time.

"Ready to do some real police work?" Pete said with a friendly smile.

He was back at his desk when I arrived. I filled him in on everything I had to date, including the news of Wilkins joining us.

"If I am, I can't help wondering if I'm I the right place," he came back with a smart reply. He was a good-natured kid and quick. "Good to see you again, Detective."

"It's Pete, okay; an' likewise." He got up and stepped over with his hand outstretched.

"Right," I said. "That's done, let's get to work. I been thinkin' 'bout this Mitchell fella. If he is stealin' documents for the Russian, he would be our best chance of findin' him, that is if we can roll him over."

"Possibly," Wilkins said, "but Commander Parks thinks it might yield better results if we could keep tabs on him; see if he leads us to more people, that's why he's sending more men down to help with any stakeout you set up."

"I see his point, an' we want to help you guys round up these traitors, but I want the Russian for the murder of Greshenko."

"We can accomplish both objectives, don't you think?"

"Yeah, I do. It's jus' that once you guys get your hands on him...?" I said.

Wilkins had no answer, so he simply shrugged his shoulders.

"Well, there's always Wallace," Pete said.

"Small consolation prize," I said, "but he'll do. How'd you make out with Morrison 'bout okayin' the allocation of manpower to our case?"

"He's okay'd it. Sez we can have two men. I already picked them out. They'll be here 'round five."

"Who?"

"Jack Findlay and Willie Jones. The other two Phil sent over are Joel Zimmerman and Calvin Lackey."

"Good choice on Findlay an' Jones." I knew both men. They were excellent cops with good instincts and lots of experience. They were also resourceful and tough buggers.

"Here's how we'll set the surveillance up."

I outlined the schedule as follows: Pete would take the first six hours with Findlay and one of Phil's men, starting at six today. Wilkins would take the second shift with Jones and one of his men in the morning. I'll work between them, following up on anything that comes in. We agreed that there was not much we could expect after midnight but decided that one of Phil's people could handle it on his own, reporting in if anything developed.

* * *

I arrived at my usual time the following morning to find Pete already in.

"Mornin'," I said, pouring out a mug of tea. "How'd it go last night?"

"Not much happened," he answered. "He went out 'round seven-thirty to a

127

boozer. Stayed there for a coupla hours then left with a woman back to her place. Left there 'round eleven-twenty for his place."

"Recognize the woman?"

"Not really. Why? It important?"

"Don't know," I said. "Remember the Russian was reportedly comin' here with a woman."

"Shit, you're right. I completely forgot 'bout that," he said, tapping his forehead with the palm of his hand. "Sorry."

"No harm done. Next time watch an' see if he comes out with her again. In the meantime, check her out. You got her address. And be discreet. Don't want to alert him we lookin' at him."

"Gotcha. By the way, refresh my memory, what was her name? This woman 'spose to've come down with the Russian."

I went to my desk and opened a file. "Celeste Dumont. It's possible she might not be usin' her real name. Here, check out the last known description the Ottawa people had for her." I passed him the file.

"Right," he said after a few moments, "I know jus' who to talk to."

He passed the file back to me.

"Okay. Let's catch up at lunch time down at the Lantern."

I was referring to the Green Lantern Restaurant on Barrington Street; a popular diner used by most everyone on the force. They offered up fairly good fare at a reasonable price.

"Okay," he said.

Just then the morning team showed up lead by Wilkins. He nodded at me then went to talk to Pete. I watched him for moment, thinking that he was on his way to becoming a first-rate detective. He would be a good addition to the force after the war. I made a mental note to put the idea to Morrison.

* * *

Mitchell stood in front of the mirror attached to his dresser, straightening his tie. He had a smile on his face as he thought about seeing Celeste again and the prospect of her naked body under him.

He stole a quick glance at his pocket watch: seven-twenty-five. He had to hurry it up. His meeting with her was set for eight o'clock and she did not like to be kept waiting.

He arrived at their usual meeting place ten minutes early; a club located at eighty-seven Hollis Street. It was not swanky or usually too crowded and the liquor was not badly watered down. There were often some local musicians playing with a small space to dance. He and Celeste would always stay for a drink or two then head back to her place.

The room was about half full with sailors, civilians, and their dates. It was quiet; the entertainment had not yet arrived. He made his way between the tables to the bar and ordered a beer for himself and a glass of rye and soda for her then took them over to an empty table in the corner to wait. He sat watching several couples dancing while he nursed his beer. When he checked his watch, he saw it read eight-twenty. She was late. By nine o'clock he knew she wasn't coming.

He finished his beer got up, leaving her whisky on the table. By the time he was back outside he was feeling frustrated and ticked off. He was really looking forward to their tryst. He flagged down a passing cab and ordered the driver to take him to her home.

The cab arrived at the address he had given just in time to see her go inside with the Russian, Petrov. They had their arms around each other. What the hell, he thought, feeling a knot grow in his gut.

"That'll be four bits," the cab driver said, looking over his shoulder.

"Huh...what?" Mitchell said, looking back at him.

"Four bits. We're here."

"Yeah...yeah, no wait. Take me back to where you picked me up."

"Jesus, mate," the driver muttered as he shifted into first gear. "Make up yer mind."

Back at the bar, Mitchell went inside and took a seat at the bar. He sat there drinking beer and going over thoughts and images about her and Petrov; all of which made him angrier with each glass of beer. After five glasses, he was definitely feeling their effect and the bartender told him he better head on out.

He staggered into his room and tossed his overcoat onto a chair then collapsed on his bed. The last thoughts running through his mind were how he was going to get even with her.

Earlier that same evening, Jack Markham sat at his desk in the electronics department located in HMC Dockyard where he was employed as an electronics technician on the navy's radar and sonar systems. He also worked in conjunction with the engineering department at the Nova Scotia Technical College.

It was just gone six o'clock and most of the workers were away home. The night shift was not due in until seven. Because of the war, his department was working around the clock. Once the last man left, he got up and went to the door of the room and checked the hall for the sentry. Security was tight because of the sensitive nature of the material he worked with. He knew he only had about twenty minutes to get the information he wanted before the patrolling guard came by.

Each time he took something from the files for the Russian, he asked himself what he had got himself into. Part of him wanted to quit, stop being a traitor. But the money he paid was too much to pass on not to mention the side benefits. He long ago decided to abandon any hope of quelling his appetites, expensive though they proved to be.

He closed the door and headed for the row of file cabinets against the back wall. He spun the button on the combination lock and opened a drawer. He flipped through the tabs until he found what he wanted. Pulling the file, he took it to his desk where he opened it and extracted several sheets of paper with schematics drawn on it then took over to the mimeograph machine to copy. He set everything up then began turning the handle, glancing quickly at the wall clock: twenty minutes to go before the guard was due.

Once more he found himself thinking about what he was doing and for a brief moment felt a pang of guilt, but then he remembered the money the Russian was willing to pay. The dosh would just about cover his outstanding markers on his gambling debts. He knew the holder of the markers would wait; he was good for them after all. But the threat of any kind of physical harm or the loss of being able to play ate at him. Then there were the girls.

When he finished rolling the last document through the machine, he peeled off the inked master and, folding it, he took it to the shedder for destruction and to be burned later.

He returned the file to the cabinet and relocked the drawer. Back at his desk, he folded the copies he made and stuffed them in the rear of his trousers, put on his overcoat and hat then went to the door. He looked around the room, making sure nothing looked out of place, then turned off the lights and stepped into the hall, locking the door behind him. The uniformed and armed guard was just rounding the corner as he walked away.

"Late night, eh?" the guard said as he walked past him.

"Yeah," Markham said, 'rush job. 'Night."

"Yeah, you too."

The guard stopped for a moment, watching him walk away. He took out a notebook and made a note of the encounter.

'Shit', Markham thought as he rounded the corner, seeing the guard writing in his book. He had forgotten the recent memo sent around by the head of security alerting everyone that from now on anybody still in the building after five o'clock would be recorded.

There was nothing he could do about that now. If questioned, he would bluff his way out of it. It was not uncommon for people to work a bit longer in order to finish an assignment.

Later that night, Markham sat in his car parked on Sackville Street beside the Public Gardens. He had made arrangements with

Petrov to meet there to trade the papers for the promised cash at nine-thirty. Suddenly, someone opened the back passenger door and got in, startling him. He spun around to see Petrov sitting in the shadowed corner.

"You have papers?" he said without preamble.

"Yeah," Markham said. "The money?"

Petrov pulled out an envelope from inside his jacket and held it up. Markham picked up the papers from the seat and passed them over, taking the envelope with his other hand. He quickly opened it to see five one-hundred-dollar bank notes inside.

"I need papers on new targeting system for main armament. You get?" he asked.

"I don't know," Markham said as he stuffed the envelope inside his jacket. "They've beefed up security. It's harder..."

"You get, I pay same price," Petrov said, interrupting him. "Also, I find some new girls for you. Just arrived from Montreal."

"I'll try. No promises. If I can find them and manage to get copies, I'll call."

"Da. Very good." Markham did not see the smile that crossed the Russian's face.

Chapter Nine

The first morning's briefings ended so I took the time to work out my next move. It was then that Jack Rawlins came in. He stopped at my desk and took a seat.

"Mornin' Jack," I said. "What's up?"

"Robie," he said, tipping his fedora back on his head. "Last night, me an' George was at the Chinaman's joint over on Argyle Street lookin' inta somethin'."

The Chinaman he referred to was a small-time restaurant operator who also ran a floating poker game out of his basement. We'd tried to shut him down but he had some connection on the City Council and managed to skate whenever we brought him in.

"I spotted one 'a my snitches. He waves me over an' sez he's got somethin' might be of interest to us. Seems Wallace has the word out he wants ta see the Indian, Kelly Johns."

"Johns ya say? Now I wonder what that's about?"

Jack shrugged, saying, "Dunno, but if he's lookin' to use him it can't be good."

Johns was well known to us. We believed he was connected to a number of unsolved assaults with bodily harm and a possible killing. He was an alcoholic who was extremely dangerous when drunk and had been known to do anything if there was enough money in it.

"Anyway, thought you otta know since Wallace's name is involved in what yer workin' on."

"Thanks. Appreciate this," I said. "By the way, who was the snitch?"

"Louie Arsenault. Why? Ya gonna talk ta him?"

"Thought I might. That a problem?"

"Not for me. He's a piece of shit but useful if ya get me."

"Yeah. Where can I find him?"

"He's usually 'round the Chinaman's place. Shills for ole man Hum." Terence Hum owned the restaurant. It was a popular place among the merchantmen and those who fancied Asian cooking.

Now I had two people to look for that, if I had a choice, I would rather not see, except to run in. There was nothing for it so, I grabbed my hat and coat and set out to find them. While I drove down to the Chinaman's place, I mulled over the tidbit of news Jack told me about Kelly Johns, trying to piece together any reason why Wallace wanted to see him. You only used Johns if you wanted to do someone serious harm. Best solution would be to pick him up and ship him out of the city, anywhere but here. Problem was we could not do that without cause and Wallace wanting him was not sufficient cause.

I spotted an empty space a few doors down from the entrance to Hum's place on Argyle Street. I pulled into the curb, turned off the motor and got out.

There were a dozen or more men standing around out front, mostly talking amiably and smoking cigarettes. They cast curious glances my way as I stepped up to them. I picked out at least four different accents: merchantmen, I reckoned. Then I spotted Arsenault.

He was a little man about five-foot-one and not much more than a hundred-and-twenty soaking wet. He was well known in town as a slippery character with a finger in a number of shady operations. He was also known, especially to us, as a valuable source of information. When he saw me, he inched his way past the men in the opposite direction.

"Hey, Louis," I called out, making my way past several of the men. "Holdup."

He stopped and turned to face me as I neared him.

"Heh, heh," he said nervously, "I didn't see ya there."

"Keep your pants on. I'm not here to roust you."

He eyed me suspiciously. "Yeah?"

"Yeah. I jus' wanna have a little chat. Let's move over there." I pointed to the entrance of an alley between two buildings, taking him by the elbow and leading him down the sidewalk. When we reached the alley, I eased him just inside.

"Whaddya want?" he said once we stopped, pulling his arm out of my hand as turned to face me.

"I hear that Wallace is lookin' for Kelly Johns," I said. "Why?"

"How da 'ell do I know what Wallace does?"

"How do you know he's lookin' for Johns?'

"I 'ear things."

"Yeah, we know. Tell me what you heard."

"Jus' dat someone was 'round lookin' fer Johns."

"How do you know Wallace wants him then?" I asked.

"Was one 'a his men that was lookin' fer him."

"An'?"

"An' dat's it," Arsenault said.

You better not be jerkin' me around."

"No way I would do dat. Ya know me, I jus' keep me ears open an' 'appy ta 'elp ya when I can."

"Yeah. You're a model citizen," I said.

"'Sides, I want nuttin' ta do with Wallace or that nutter Johns."

"Okay. You hear anythin' 'bout Johns you call me, got it?"

"Yeah. Got it. We done now?"

"Yeah," I said, stepping aside. "Take off."

He eased past me and hot-footed it back to his place outside the restaurant.

I headed back to my car and for my next call: Charlie Roode. I checked my watch: eleven-thirty, time to meet up with Pete at the Green Lantern Restaurant. Roode could wait until later, besides it was unlikely he would be drinking this early.

I spotted Pete sitting at the counter drinking a coffee and made my way through several sailors standing around the entrance. The waitress saw me when I stepped inside and lifted a coffee pot. I nodded.

"Been awhile, Robie," she said setting a mug on the countertop as I took the empty stool next to my friend.

"Hi Rose," I said, "it has. How're ya doin'?"

"You know, a girl's gotta keep the boys happy." She said this with a smile and a twinkle in her eye as she tilted her head at the swarm of young men.

Rose Kennedy was an attractive thirty something woman with a well-proportioned figure and nice looking legs which she enjoyed flaunting to the roving eyes of

139

hungry young men. However, she was also a married woman with two kids at home. Like so many women in her circumstance, she took a job to make ends meet. And had been at the Lantern for the last two years.

Her old man was in the army and currently somewhere in Italy. We'd known each other for a few years now and I 'd never known her to take up with anyone.

"How're the kids?"

"Kids is kids," she said. "And yours?"

I smiled and said, "Kids is kids."

"Say hi to Louise for me."

"Will do, thanks." I watched appreciatively as she walked away. Like I said; nice legs.

"Anything interestin'?" I asked, turning to Pete who was also watching her.

"Not too much, you?"

"Rawlins came in this morning and told me that one of his snitches passed on somethin'. Seems like Wallace is lookin' for Kelly Johns."

"Christ," Pete said. "What the hell he want with that crazy sonofabitch?"

"No idea, but whatever it is won't be good."

"So, whaddya we gonna do 'bout him? Pick him up?"

"On what charge? No, I don't think we'd get away with jus' arrestin' him. All the same, make it a priority to find out where he is an' let's keep tabs on him."

"Okay."

"You see Wilkins today?" I asked.

"No, he was gone when I came in," Pete said.

"How're Phil's people workin' out?"

"Don't know 'bout the one with Wilkins but the one with me seems to know his stuff. He sez he was a cop before the war up in Oshawa, Ontario. His name is Joel Zimmerman. Pleasant enough fella."

"Good." I picked up my mug, took a drink. "Let's eat."

I waved to Rose who came over.

Later, I was parked outside Bill Clark's place on Garrish Street, watching the small group of men milling about on the sidewalk. Most were young sailors too young to get in the legitimate drinking places. The bootleggers didn't much care if they weren't of age as long as they behaved themselves. Two black men were standing near the door.

I saw Roode as he rounded the corner from Creighton Street and made his way to the boozer. I opened the door and got out, crossing the street to intercept him. About half-way across the street he saw me and came to a halt.

"Don't even think about it," I called out to him just as he looked like he was about to turn tail and run off. He paused long enough for me to reach him.

"Whaddya want? I ain't done nuttin'," he protested when I reached him and grabbed his elbow.

"You're comn' with me," I said. "Let's go."

We were almost to the car when someone called out, "Hey, Charlie. Ya okay? What's goin' on?"

I walked us past the front of the car, opened the passenger door, and shoved him inside. Turning, I saw a couple of men, including one of the black men head for the car. I quickly pulled my wallet and flashed my badge.

"Back away," I ordered threateningly.

As soon as they saw my badge they stopped; one of them throwing up his hands and shaking his head as he stepped back. I got in and started the motor. I pulled away toward Gottingen Street then turned south at the corner.

"What da 'ell dis about?" Roode said, sounding nervous. "I ain't done nuttin'. Ya can't jus' roust me like dis."

"I hear ya been workin' for a Russian," I said, ignoring his complaint.

"Wh...what'd ya say? How'd ya...," he said before he realized he let the cat out of the bag. "I don't know what yer talkin' 'bout. I don't know no Russians."

"Can it. Word is you been shootin' your mouth off about some bad shit you witnessed." I was shooting in the dark here, but I could see he was rattled and I had a hunch he wasn't a hard case. So, leaning on him might work.

"I got nuttin' ta say," he said defiantly.

"We'll see 'bout that. Maybe some time in the cells at Naval Intelligence will loosen your tongue."

"Whaddya mean, Naval Intelligence? Wot dey gotta do with this?"

"They're interested in the Russian. I was asked to pick you up."

"Whaddya mean, fer Chrissake? Whaddya dey want wit me?"

"Dunno, but once I turn you over it's outta my hands. And when they got you, there'll be no lawyers or anythin' like that."

"They can't do dat. It ain't legal; I got rights."

"Not in wartime you don't, especially when it comes to intelligence."

I was really pushing my luck, but I figured he would not have any idea about what I was saying, and he looked close to breaking.

"Jesus," he said, obviously distraught. "Look. Can we do a deal; you an' me?"

"Like what? I mean, I can't disobey my orders, ya know." I said as we drove through the intersection at Cogswell and Brunswick Streets.

"I got information might be useful to ya."

"Like what?"

"Like maybe I know this Russian yer innnerested in. Like maybe I see'd him kill a fella."

"The Navy people already know that."

"Yeah? How 'bout dey know dis Russian is stealin' secrets?"

"How do you know that?"

"Wallace's workin' for him, see. Put him in touch wit' people work in da shipyard and dockyard."

"Good boy," I said. "Go on."

"Dat's it," he said. "Dat's all I knows."

"Yeah? How come you know this much, eh?"

"I bin drivin' da bastard 'round."

"So ya know where he lives then?"

"Naw. 'E calls da boss an' he sends me to pick 'im up at different places."

"You got the names of these men Wallace has given him?"

"Only one I 'eard was sum fella name of Jack Markham."

"Markham? That it?"

"Uh-huh," Roode said, nodding. "Look, I bin good 'ere, yeah? So, whaddya say?"

"Okay," I said, easing over to the curb across from St. Mathews church on Barrington Street. "But from now on I own you, understand?"

"Yeah." He sounded dejected and beaten.

"From now on you're to call me whenever Wallace sends you out, clear?"

"Yeah."

"Good. Now get out."

As he opened his door, he turned to look at me and said, "Dat mean no Navy people?"

"Yeah," I said, 'for now', I thought to myself. After all, Wallace and his people were engaged in espionage and, besides, Roode was just another lowlife that'd be better off the streets.

I looked over my left shoulder then eased out the clutch and continued on down to Naval Headquarters. I wanted to have a quick chat with Phil and let him know about Jack Markham.

"And you say this Roode character told you there was a someone positioned in the shipyard that is working with or for the Russian?" Michael Parks asked when I arrived twenty minutes later.

"So he says, yeah," I said.

"And you believe him?"

"It don't matter if I believe him, does it? It's enough that he's given up a name of someone who could be a security risk at the very least if not in direct contact with the Russian."

"Point taken. So, how do you suggest we proceed?" he asked Phil who sat behind his desk.

"We could put a man on this Markham or just bring him in," he said.

"I don't think that would be a good idea at this point," I said.

Both men looked at me.

"Sure, you might plug a possible security leak if you bring Markham in but that doesn't bring us any closer to getting' the Russian an' that's what is the main objective, right?"

"True," Michael said. "But we cannot permit the leaking of secret documents to continue; that must take priority."

"I understand that," I said. Then I had a thought. "How 'bout this. You have your people keep eyes on Markham while he's on the job and take him in the act of stealin' the documents; catch him with his hand in the cookie jar, so to speak. Then, when you have him dead to rights, bring him in an' sweat him into workin' with us. I'd stake my pension on him leadin' us right to the Russian."

"You know that just might work," Phil said.

"God, you have a devious mind," Michael added. "I'm glad you are on our side. You sure you wouldn't like to transfer over to intelligence? You are a natural."

"No thanks," I said. "Bein' a cop is good enough for me. All I gotta deal with are villains."

They both chuckled a bit at that remark.

"Right. I'll leave it to you to set this up," he said to Phil. "Thank you again Robie."

"No   problem."

Chapter Ten

When I arrived the next morning, Willie Jones and another man stood in front of my desk now occupied by Carl Wilkins. The man must have been one of Phil's men sent down to help out.

"Right," Wilkins said, looking up at the two men. "You've been briefed so you know what's required here."

"Yeah," Jones said. "We're 'spose to keep this fella, Mitchell, under surveillance. Keep track of where he goes an' who he talks to."

"That's it. We're interested in finding a Russian agent and believe this guy is working for him. It's possible he's also in touch with a French woman from Quebec who's suspected of being connected to the Russian. Her name is Celeste Dumont. We need to find out where she's at."

"What if we find this Russian? You want us to pick him up?"

"No. Report back to either me or Robie. Whatever you do don't brace him. This man is a killer and should be treated as very dangerous, got it?"

"Got it."

"Okay," Wilkins said. "Here's my plan. Phelan here has a security pass that'll get him into the yard, so he'll go in an' pick up Mitchell, keepin' tabs on his movements in the yard. You hang back outside in the car which you'll park near the gate."

"Guess I better put up a sandwich an' a jug a coffee," Findlay said, chuckling.

"Don't worry too much about that," Wilkins said. "I'll spell you during the day. Just stand by in case Mitchell leaves the yard then you and Phelan stay with him."

"Gotcha," Findlay said.

"How far do you want me to stick to him while he's in the dockyard?" Zimmerman asked. "There'll be rovin' patrols of SPs an' others who might note my presence."

"As far as you can without blowin' your cover, I suppose. Use your own judgment. If someone stops you jus' show them your ID but say nothin' 'bout why you're there."

"Yeah, that'd work I 'spose."

"Right. You better get goin'. Call in if somethin' happens," Wilkins said, then turning to Jones said, "I'll try an' get down 'round noon to relieve you for an hour or so. Good luck." The two officers headed out of the squad room.

"Sorry about taking your desk," Wilkins said, standing up.

"No problem," I said, moving around the desk and took my seat. "Sounds like you got a good plan there."

"Thanks."

"I take it that other fella with Jones is one 'a yours?"

"Yeah. His name's Kevin Phelan. A good man. Been with the service since the start."

"Cop?"

"Mountie. Three years up in Manitoba."

I nodded my understanding.

"Well, if you got nothing for me I think I'll stop down at the office and see if anything new has come in."

"Right," I said. "Let's talk again later."

I watched him as he headed out.

A couple of hours later, Pete and Jack Findlay came into the squad room.

"Mornin'," I said.

"Mornin'," Pete answered as Findlay just nodded and headed for an empty desk.

"How'd it go last night?"

"Not much. He left his place 'round eight an' went to a boozer up on Creighton Street. Stayed for 'bout an hour then headed back to his place."

"No sign of the woman?"

"Not that we saw."

"What's the plan for tonight?" I asked.

"Depends on what happens today an' what Wilkins finds out I reckon. Otherwise, it's pretty much the same as last night. I'll leave it to Findlay an' Zimmerman. I'll hang in here in case they need me."

149

"Okay."

"How 'bout you? Any luck?"

"I found Roode an' had a chat with him."

"Anythin' interestin'?"

"Wallace is definitely workin' for the Russian. Looks like Roode is drivin' him around. Accordin' to Roode, the Russian has a coupla pigeons providin' him with information. Plus, I think he was a witness to the Greshenko killin'."

"Jesus," Pete said, whistling. "He say where he lives?"

"Unfortunately, no. This guy's no dummy. Looks like he calls Wallace whenever he needs a ride, tellin' him where to send Roode and the car. Our best chance to findin' him is to hope that Mitchell leads us to him or the woman. I gotta a hunch she knows where he's holed up."

"So, how long you gonna let Wallace run loose?"

"Not much longer," I said. "I got him on a leash now an' I wanna see what else I can shake loose before I pick him up."

"Anythin' new on this Johns business?" Pete asked.

"Not yet," I said shaking my head. "I'm a bit concerned 'bout his name poppin' up right now. He a bad one an' dangerous. I'd really like to find out why Wallace wants him."

"Yeah. I had a run in with him a while back." Pete instinctively placed a hand on his jaw and started rubbing it.

"I remember. Right. You got your team set for tonight. Why don't you an' Findlay take the afternoon off an' get some rest."

"Thanks, we will."

"By the way, how's Zimmerman workin' out?"

"Good man, actually. He said he was goin' to report in at headquarters this mornin', that's why he's not here. I'll give him a quick call to fill him in on tonight."

"Right," I said and watched him walk away back to his desk.

The rest of the day passed with the usual headaches we normally dealt with on a daily basis. I took the time to get caught up on what the rest of the squad was working on.

Later that night, at home, Pete called. It was close to eleven o'clock and I had only just turned in.

Robichaud," I said when I answered the call. I had a phone installed beside the bed back in forty-one.

"Bad news." It was Pete. He was down at Naval Headquarters with Phil. "You better get down here."

"Right," I said, "On my way. Be there in ten minutes, traffic permitting."

"What is it, dear?" my wife, Louise, asked sleepily.

151

"Cop stuff," I answered, kissing her on the cheek. "Back to sleep, now. I hafta go."

"Be careful. Love you."

"Love you too, pet."

It took almost twenty minutes to get down. I ran into an army transport convoy heading for the embarkation area at the ocean terminals. I wasn't sure if it carried men destined for the beachheads in France or war materials. It did not matter since both were in great demand now that the Allies were fighting in Europe.

"What's up?" I said when I stepped into the room set aside for us. Phil and Michael were already sitting at the table; Pete was also there. He did not look too good.

"One of Pete's team is missing," Phil said without any preamble.

"What! Missing how?" I said, taking a chair.

"Pete," Michael said, looking at my partner.

"I got a call from Findlay," he started, looking at me. "As near as I can make out from what he reported, they were following Mitchell as planned when he ended up down on Church Street. He stopped at one of the houses and started to bang on the door. After several minutes a woman appeared and an argument broke out; it ended with her slappin' him across the face then goin' back inside, slammin' the door." He paused for a moment.

"Yeah, go on," I said.

"Then Mitchell took off down the street towards South," Pete said, continuing his account. "Findlay said they agreed to split up, with him following Mitchell, an' Zimmerman hangin' back to watch the house. He sez he followed Mitchell to that tavern across from the Waverley and went in. Then he headed back to get Zimmerman. It was when he reached the spot where Zimmerman was 'spose to be that he spotted his body. His throat was cut."

"Jesus, Mary and Joseph," I said.

"Anyway, he hot-footed it back to the car and called it in."

"Did dispatch send anybody down there?"

"No. He told the duty officer to put him directly through to me. I made the call to not send anybody 'til we had a chance to talk."

"Good...good, you did right," I said. I turned my gaze to Michael. "This is getting' outta hand. I can't, won't, let this go on, Michael. We gotta think about roundin' the lotta them up before someone else is killed."

"I understand your concerns, Robie, but..." he started to say.

"No buts, here. Morrison and the mayor are gonna go off the deep end when they hear about this."

"What's the best we can hope to gain if we act now?" Michael said with a sense of urgency in his voice. "A second-rate criminal? Maybe a French agitator? A

153

couple of possible traitors?" He leaned forward, resting his arms on the table.

"The man responsible for the killing of one of *my* men and the Greshenko brother will still be at large, possibly plotting more killing."

"I realize that for Chrissake," I said. "I'm jus' tellin' you what to expect from my side when this comes to light. I understand your point an' for the most part, I agree with you. I want to get this bastard jus' as badly as you."

"I know," he said, contritely. "I was not suggesting anything otherwise."

"If I may suggest something," Phil said, stepping into the conversation.

"Yes?" Michael said, looking to his colleague.

"I don't think we should hold off sending in the police to investigate what happened down on Church Street. After all, I wouldn't be surprised if there hasn't already been calls from people who live there. Besides, it'll give us the opportunity to look into the house where Mitchell stopped and had the confrontation with a woman, who I think we can assume is the Quebecer."

"You do not honestly think she will still be there, do you?" Michael asked.

"Probably not," I cut in. "But we'd have a reason to look at her room an' talk to the landlord about visitors an' such. If he was there an' with her then they've likely taken off an' in a hurry. That means..."

"They might have left something behind," Michael said, finishing what I was going to say. "Clever. Right then, I will leave this business to you, as it is obviously in your bailiwick. I will call the mayor's office in the morning and advise him of our situation, and the need to keep you and Pete in place here for a bit longer. By the way, Phil. Did Zimmerman have any family?"

"I'll look into it and make the necessary arrangements."

"Thank you." He stood up and left the three of us alone.

"He's lookin' tired," I said, after he was gone.

"Who isn't these days," Phil said.

"No kiddin'," Pete said.

"What now?" Phil asked.

"Pete and I will head up to Church Street. First though, I'll call it in an' have dispatch round up the crime scene boys to meet us down there. I'll have then contact Findlay to stand by 'til we get there."

"I'll check in after we're done. Hopefully, we'll catch a break," I said, as we both stood up.

"That'd make a nice change," Phil said sourly.

I didn't envy his next job.

* * *

Earlier that night.

Larry Mitchell left his work in the Dockyard at six forty-five and headed for Barrington Street. Findlay saw him pass through the security gate followed a few minutes later by Zimmerman, who was heading for the car.

They sat watching their man standing with several other workmen waiting for the next tram to come by.

They pulled out of the parking area and managed to get in behind the tram, keeping at least five cars back. Luckily, the traffic was not too heavy just at that time of the evening.

Mitchell finally disembarked the tram beside St Paul's Church near the corner at Prince Street. He turned up Prince. Findlay stopped the car near the curb long enough for Zimmerman get out and follow on foot. He would follow in the car.

Mitchell walked up to Grafton Street where he lived. He went inside and re-emerged twenty minutes later wearing a fresh change of clothes.

Zimmerman watched for Findlay and the car. When he saw it turn the corner, he crossed over as Findlay parked the car and got in. He pointed out the house Mitchell lived in.

It was now close to eight-thirty when Mitchell exited the house. He headed south toward Spring Garden Road then turned down Queen Street, heading for Morris

Street. Findlay stayed back, keeping his eyes on Mitchell who wore a heavy tan coloured wool greatcoat; his head covered with a fedora.

It was dark but the streetlights were on. The ban on lights after dark had been relaxed a while back, so it was easy enough to follow him in spite of the traffic and passing pedestrians. They saw him turn down Morris then onto Church Street. They stopped at the corner because it was a one-way street and there wasn't any traffic moving there. They didn't want to alert him of their presence. Zimmerman got out and went to the corner of a building and watched. Five minutes later he climbed back in.

"Christ, it's bloody cold out there. Looks like he had a run in with a woman," he said, closing the door. "They were yelling at each other then she smacked him in the face then went back inside, slamming the door. He took off cussin' like a stevedore."

"Which way?" Findlay asked.

"Towards South Street. I seen him turn down Harvey."

"Right. I think for now we split up. You know the house he stopped at?"

"Yeah, I think so."

"Good. Point it out an' I'll let you out close by. You go check it out while I go after him an' see where he's headin'. There ain't much down that part of Barrington 'cept for a tavern. Chances are he's headin' there.

Soon as I'm sure I'll double back and pick you up."

"Okay."

Findlay drove down the street slowly and when Zimmerman pointed out the house, he eased to the curb. Zimmerman got out, and as soon as he closed his door, Findlay pulled away heading for the corner of Harvey Street.

He spotted Mitchell quick enough and saw him approach Barrington Street close to the Waverley Inn. When he reached the bottom of Harvey, he saw him cross over and enter the tavern. He drove to the intersection at Morris and turned left. When he arrived on Church, he didn't see Zimmerman anywhere.

Pulling the car over to the curb near where he left Zimmerman, he put it in first and shut off the motor still looking out the window. Then he spotted it; feet sticking out from the darkened narrow alley between two houses. He quickly got out of the car and hurried across the street with his gun in hand. It was the body of a man lying face down in the snow that piled up the sides of the buildings. Then he saw the black stain under the body's head.

He took a step into the alley and bent down. A knot tightened in his gut as he reached for the victim's shoulder to turn him over knowing what he would find. He slowly lifted the shoulder enough to recognize the body: it was Zimmerman. His throat was cut. Findlay stood, pressing his back against the wall, choking back the bile rising in his throat. It was then that he saw the ragged trail of blood in the snow leading from the alley. He automatically followed it with his eyes, ending a couple doors down. The kill spot.

Getting his calm back, he dashed across to the car, got in, and reached for the microphone attached to the two-way radio.

* * *

"What was that all about?" Petrov asked when Celeste came back into the room.

"Mitchell," she said. "He was here and wanted to come in. I said no and he became angry. I hit him and told him to stay away from me."

"I will talk to him."

"No. Leave him alone. You have too much attention already."

"As you wish, *lastachka*," he said, calling her by one of his pet names.

"By the way, I thought I saw a car down at the end of the street with two men inside."

"Da?"

"It might be nothing," she said.

He got up and went for his overcoat.

"Where are you going?"

"To check," he said. "Wait here. Get ready in case."

He left the room and headed for the stairs then, once at the bottom, headed for the back door. When they took the rooms, he scouted the area for escape routes, so he was able to make his way through the several backyards, checking the alleyways between the houses as he went. Then he saw the shadowed figure of a man standing at the end of an alley two houses down from where they stayed.

He pulled out his knife, opening the long, razor-sharp blade and crept silently towards the man. When he reached him, he quickly grabbed him around the face, tilting his head back enough to expose the throat then, with a fast powerful stroke, pulled the blade across, cutting deep into the neck.

He heard a startled gurgling sound as the blade exited then felt the body sag under his arm. He slowly pulled the dead man into the alley, laying his body on the snow-covered ground. He quickly checked the street then turned and headed back to the room.

"We must go...now!" he said when he closed the door behind him. He went back into the hall and went to the wall phone. He called Wallace and told him to send a car, giving him the location of the place to go. When he got back to the room, Celeste stood with her coat on and with two small Gladstone fabric bags beside her.

He took one last look around, then they left, moving quietly to the stairs.

Chapter Eleven

I saw Findlay standing next to his car and pulled in behind it. As Pete and I got out, Findlay pointed to the alley where Zimmerman's body lay.

"Pete," I said, nodding in the direction of the body. "Take a look."

"Yeah," he said, a hint of anger in his voice.

"How ya doin', Jack?" I asked as I approached the detective. He was staring at the ground.

"I ain't never seen anythin' like that before," he said in a shaky voice. "What kinna animal does somethin' like that to another human being? Jesus."

"You up to tellin' me what happened?"

"Yeah, I'll try."

"Good man. Let's sit in the car, okay? It's colder than a witch's heart out here."

After we settled in the car, he took out a pack of Black Cat's and lit one up.

I said, "Okay. In your own time."

"We picked him up at the dockyard an' followed him home," Findlay began. "He left again 'round eight-thirty. We followed him down to Church Street where he had a set-to with some woman then he took off. Zimmerman stayed back to check out the house while I follow him down to Barrington. I seen him go in that tavern across from the Waverley, ya know the one. Then I high tailed it back to pick up Zimmerman. That's when I found him."

That it?" I asked when he stopped talking. "You saw no one else?"

"That's it."

After a brief moment, I said," Look, I appreciate you talkin' to me an' I see this has shaken' you up pretty bad, so why don't you pack it in an' go home. We can pick this up again in the mornin' at the station."

"Yeah...yeah, thanks, Robie. I need a stiff drink an' there's a quart a good rye at home," he said.

"Good. Go home an' get drunk. See ya in the mornin'."

I got out and watched as he drove off then turned and headed for where Pete was still part way into the alley. I heard a siren in the distance as I reached him.

"Whaddya got?" I asked.

"We gotta get this son of a bitch, Robie" he snarled, looking up at me. "Poor bastard probably didn't even feel a thing. Whatever cut him was razor sharp. Looks like it cut a good three maybe four inches into the throat. Looks a lot like the cut made on Greshenko."

"Christ," I said, absentmindedly making the sign of the cross. "When ya called for the crime scene fellas, did you also call for an ambulance? I wanna get him outta there as soon as possible."

"Yeah, they should be here in a few minutes."

"We'll wait 'till the men show up then pay a visit to the house Mitchell stopped at. I gotta feelin' we're gonna find that was where the French woman was livin' an' maybe even the Russian."

"They won't still be there...would they?"

"Not likely. But be ready all the same. If he is still there, he won't come easy," I said. "An' don't underestimate the woman."

"Okay," Pete said, standing up still looking down at the fallen officer.

A few moments later the ambulance turned the corner followed a minute later by a squad car with the crime scene team. Once they secured the area and I filled them in on what we knew so far, I signaled for Pete to follow me.

We went to the door of the house Findlay pointed out and I banged on it a few times. Several moments passed before a disgruntled old man opened the door.

"Whaddya want? Ya know what time it is fer Chrissake?" he grumbled.

"Police," I said, taking a step forward.

"Whoa there, matey, what's this about, eh?" He suddenly woke up.

"We know you got a Frenchwoman rentin' here. We want to see her room."

"You can't just come bargin' into my home like this," he protested. "Besides, I think she's gone. Her and that big foreigner fella."

"Whaddya mean gone," Pete said, his tone hard. He was still burning with anger. "How do ya know that?"

"I was in bed, and I heard them in the hall. Sounded like they was in hurry."

"Did they have a car?" I asked.

"Not that I ever noticed."

"Right. Which was her room?"

"Upstairs. First on the right."

Pete was already on the stair leading up. I fell in behind him.

The door was still slightly ajar, so Pete pushed it in with his foot. I saw that he had drawn his pistol. The room was empty, although I detected the faint floral scent of the woman's perfume.

It wasn't much as rooms went. An open spacious area with a sofa, chair and a wooden table against the wall next to an icebox. A kitchenette was set up against one wall. There was a door which opened onto a small toilet. The other door led into the bedroom. They obviously took off in a great hurry since a lot of her stuff was still here. I also spotted several items that must have belonged to the Russian.

"Check the bedroom," I said to Pete, seeing him put the gun back into its holster.

"Maybe they left some papers or something. I check out here."

Ten minutes later we finished searching the flat and headed back downstairs. The landlord, now dressed in a pair of woolen work pants with suspenders hanging down the sides and a loose shirt, stood at the bottom.

"What's that you're takin'?" he demanded, eyeing the items I held in my hand.

"Nothin' that concerns you," I snapped. "An' one more thing, stay outta the rooms up there. They're part of a police crime scene. If you go up there, you'll be arrested. Clear?"

"You can't stop me from goin' anywhere in my own house."

"Your choice, mate, but I'm leavin' orders with my men out there to arrest you or anyone else goes into those rooms."

Pete had already headed outside. I turned on my heel and followed him outside. I spoke to one of the crime scene men, a fella named Johnson, an' told him when he was done here to go up and check out the flat.

"Let's go," I said to Pete as I headed for the car.

"Where we goin'?" he asked.

"Me, I'm goin' home and try to get a few hours sleep. There's not much more we can do tonight, besides I wanna wait an' see if the crime lads find anythin'. Wouldn't hurt you none to do the same."

"I don't know how much sleep I'll get," Pete said as I started the car, "I'm wound up too tight right now."

"All the more reason to hit the bed; try an' let some of that anger out."

"Yeah, I 'spose you're right."

"We'll meet at headquarters in the mornin' say, round about seven-thirty."

"Sounds goods."

I dropped him at his place. He and his wife, Aggie, rented a small house up on Allen Street near Monastery Lane. Then I swung the car around and headed home.

Headquarters, first thing tomorrow. I thought Phil might wanna have a look at some of these papers I found stuffed under a cushion on the sofa."

* * *

The black two door Ford sedan cruised west down South Street. Celeste Dumont and Nikolai Petrov sat in the back using the darkness to obscure them in case anyone was looking.

"Where to?" Roode asked, nervously.

"Edinburgh Street," Dumont said.

"*Mon Deux*," she said, lowering her voice. "How did they find us so quick?"

"I do not know," Petrov said. He had taken out the knife he used to dispatch the man in the alley and began to absently clean it with his handkerchief. When done, he folded the blade and put it back inside his jacket. "This policeman, he is good."

"What now?"

"We go to second location, and I call Wallace, see if he have information I need on this policeman yet."

"So, you intend to go ahead with your plan to remove this man?"

"*Da*. No choice. Especially now he gets too close."

"*Je comprends*," she said, "but you still will not consider leaving this place? You have enough information, *oui*?"

"I must obtain more," he said. "Orders."

"Order's," she snapped. "Damn these orders. It is becoming too dangerous. We must leave before you are caught."

"Do not worry. They cannot arrest me.'

"You trust too much this diplomatic immunity. They might not be able to arrest you, but they can shoot you."

"These people do not have, how they say, uh, stomach to kill me."

"I would not put too much faith in that idea. The *Anglais* are bastards and will kill anyone they do not like. I know."

"I am not so easy to kill."

Memories of St. Petersburg in the early years of the Revolution came to his mind and the dangers he faced back then, where almost anyone he encountered wanted to kill him, but he survived while many others rested now in unmarked graves.

"Let us hope so. *Merde*," Celeste Dumont said as Roode maneuvered the car around a stopped tram, picking up and discharging passengers. "How in God's name did they find us so soon?"

"Good question," Petrov said. He sat next to her staring out the side window. "I think maybe you are right. It may be time to re-consider our situation here."

"Good. It is not a nice city, not like home. I do not like the people here. Too much greed, anger. When will we go?"

"Soon. I need to get a few more items, then we can leave."

"*Bon.*"

Roode turned right onto Robie Street and headed north They were heading for the home of a party member sent to Halifax a few years ago to try and raise support among the French communities for the cause. It was located in the west end of the city on Edinburgh Street; a house owned by a man named Marcel Piaf, a French separatist.

"I am sorry you had to leave your possessions," Petrov said.

"It is a small matter," Dumont said. "I can always get more and better ones once we leave here.

"This place we go to, it is safe, *da*?"

"*Oui*. Piaf is a dedicated member of the movement. He will provide us with all we need."

"Good."

They arrived at the Piaf residence about fifteen minutes later. It was now close to midnight and the house was dark. Dumont told Roode to pull into the darkened driveway, stopping as far from the street as it allowed. She and Petrov got out.

Petrov went to the driver's door and told Roode to take off and tell Wallace he would call him in the morning. Then he went to the rear of the house behind Celeste. She stepped over to a garbage can and moved it aside where there was large rock. She tilted it back, exposing a skeleton key. She picked it up and opened the back door. They stepped into the darkened house.

"It is safe to leave key out like this?" Petrov asked in a puzzled tone.

"I was told it would be there if we needed to get inside," she answered as if this explained everything.

Once inside, she found the light switch and flipped it on. They were in a kitchen; there was a wood burning stove, icebox, small table with three chairs and several cupboards on the wall.

"Sit," she said as she headed for the door leading into a narrow hall.

She stopped at the bottom of a stairwell and, looking up, called out, "Marcel! *C'est moi;* Celeste."

A few moments later, she heard someone moving around upstairs then a door opened and a man called down, "Celeste?"

"*Oui, et Petrov.*"

"I'll be down in a moment," he called down in English, knowing the Russian did not speak much French.

She went back to the kitchen to find Petrov lighting the stove.

"Ah, good," she said. "You sit. I will make the tea. Marcel will be down in a moment." She headed for one of the cupboards looking for the tea.

"This Marcel," Petrov said. "He will help?"

"Yes, my love. He is a friend. He will let us stay here until you are ready to leave."

"And no one knows this place?"

"No one knows. It is his house. He has lived here for some time."

"What does he do here?"

"Spreads the word about the movement."

Just then they both heard footsteps from the hall. Marcel Piaf entered the kitchen dressed in woolen pajamas and a well-worn housecoat. He was in his fifties with graying hair and unshaven.

"Ah, Marcel," Celeste said, turning from the sink where she was filling the kettle from the faucet. "This is Nikolai Petrov. *Cheri*, Marcel." The two men shook hands.

"I take it there's a problem?" Marcel said in perfect English.

"Yes. We have been exposed. The police are looking for us."

"The police?"

"*Oui*. Unfortunately, Nikolai had to take drastic steps."

"Drastic steps? You mean he's injured or killed someone, right?"

She nodded, but said nothing, not wanting to go into specific details. Piaf looked from her to the Russian for a moment then sat down.

"So?," he said. "What is your plan now?"

"I must stay a few days more," Petrov said, speaking at last. "I have mission for my country, and it is here."

"So, this has nothing to do with the movement?" he said, looking back to Celeste.

"No," she said, "but they are aware of his mission and have agreed to help him."

Interesting," Piaf said. "I wonder how helping him serves the movement?"

"We support your cause," Petrov said. "When war over, we will recognize the justice of your cause."

"For all the good that'll do. But that's not my concern. How long do plan to stay?"

"Like I said, a few more days," Petrov said. He did not like this man and the contempt he implied for his government.

"And we will not draw any attention to you," Celeste hurriedly added.

"Okay. Three days then you're out of here. I have worked too long and hard to build up support among our compatriots in the city and province to risk getting found out. Agreed?"

Celeste looked at Petrov who nodded then said. "Agreed."

* * *

Mitchell sat on the edge of his single bed, staring at his bare feet. He was still feeling pissed off at how the French bitch had treated him, laughed at him, after everything he gave her; did for her. Memories of him standing there in the street looking at her as she yelled at him and the sight of the Russian standing behind her in the hall, fueled the fire burning in his gut.

He picked up his wristwatch and looked at the time: seven-fifteen. He should be getting dressed for work but not this morning. This morning his mind was consumed with devising a scheme to strike at the two of them...especially her.

Later, after he finished his breakfast and was cleaning up, he started to work on a plan.

The first step was to head for the Green Lantern cafe where she worked. He would find out the name of her boss then make an anonymous call telling them that she was using her job to offer her sexual services to their customers. Then he would make another call to the police telling them the same thing, adding that she was using her rooms on Church Street as the place where she took the johns. That would stitch her up plenty, he thought.

When he arrived at the canteen, he looked inside to make sure she was not there, then went in. He left five minutes later with the information he wanted.

He found a drugstore and asked if they had a payphone.

When he finished, he stepped outside and stood for a moment on the sidewalk. Passersby took no notice of him or the smug grin on his face as they moved past him; some making rude remarks.

Chapter Twelve

The next morning Pete and I arrived at the station about the same time. I wanted to see if the report from the crime scene men was in, as well as Findlay's report, before heading down to Headquarters and talking to Phil and Michael.

"Feelin' better?" I asked as Pete joined me at the coffee table.

"Yeah, some, thanks," he said. "You were right. Aggie was the medicine I needed."

"That's a good woman you got there, buddy."

"Don't hafta tell me. So, what's on the table for today?"

"I wanna wait on the crime scene report as well as Findlay's report. Then we'll head down an' have a talk with Phil an' Michael. Besides, I wanna take a closer look at those documents I found in the sofa."

"Okay," he said and went to his desk. I saw him pick up a couple of pieces of paper then reach for his phone. After a few minutes he hung up and came over to my desk.

"Mike Butler called in last night said he needed to talk to me. I jus' spoke to him. He wants to meet me. If it's okay, I'll take off an' see what he's got then meet you down at Headquarters."

"Yeah, okay," I said. "See there."

I turned back to the documents I had taken from the woman's room. There were five pages in all, each stamped, TOP SECRET across the top. Two were technical drawings of what looked like a long gun; the others were notes and formulas. These will definitely be of interest to Michael, I thought as I folded the pages and put them in my coat pocket.

I was slipping into my overcoat when the duty officer called.

"Robie," he said when I picked up the phone. "It's me, Ernie, out front. Some fella named Taylor is standin' here wantin' to see ya."

"Okay, thanks," I said. "Send him on through."

A few minutes later, Gerry Taylor entered the squad room. He stopped in the doorway a moment then, seeing me, came over.

"Gerry," I said, sitting on the corner of my desk. "What's up that brings you in this early?" He works as a barman and bouncer at a tavern down the south end of Barrington Street.

"I heard someone got killed last night," he said, "one a yours, as I hear it."

I sat looking at him, waiting.

"Anyway, one 'a the blokes that drink at the place I work, comes in real late an' orders a drink. Accordin' to him he's mates with the fella owns the house where the killin' happened. He sez he knows who did it an' some other shit."

"Now why would this fella come in an' start to shoot his mouth off like that, eh?"

"He's a big mouth. Likes to sound like he's in with some bad people and has connections. Ya know the type; all gas. Normally, I jus' blow him off but then I remember you askin' questions 'bout some Russian an' thought this might be connected."

"Thanks. I appreciat it." I fished my wallet out and extracted a ten-dollar banknote and handed it to him. "Now go home; get some sleep."

He thanked me then left.

Looked like I was heading back to Church Street after I met with Phil and Michael, I thought, as I headed for the parking area. Time to lean on that landlord.

I was the first to arrive at Headquarters. I knocked on Phil's office door, as his secretary was not at her desk.

"Come," he called out, then as I opened the door and stepped in, he said, "Morning. You're in early."

"Mornin'," I said as I took a chair. "Somethin's come up that you and Michael need to see. He in yet, by the way?" It was a silly question since I knew the man was always here before five. I sometimes thought he should just have a cot installed.

Phil reached for his phone. After a moment he reached him and asked him to join us in the meeting room.

"He'll be right down," Phil said as he hung up. "You go across, I'll join you in a couple of minutes."

I got up and left. I bumped into the pretty young WAVE officer who was his secretary as she was coming in.

"Oh?" she said, surprised. "I'm so sorry."

"No bother," I said with a smile. "How're you this cold November mornin'?"

"Fine, Detective, thank you." She smiled as I sidestepped to allow her through the door. "Are you meeting next door?"

"Uh-huh."

"Then I best be getting the coffee set up. It isn't usually made this early."

"Thanks. By the way, can call down an' see if the canteen can send up some warm scones or biscuits? I'm feelin' a bit peckish."

"Yes sir, certainly."

"Look, you can call me Robie...when nobody's listenin'," I said.

"Yes sir, uh, Robie," she said hesitantly. I saw it was hard for her to break with the formality she was taught.

I stepped away to the closed door directly opposite Phil's office and opened it then went inside. Phil joined me a few minutes later and took a seat at the table opposite me.

"What's the latest?" he asked. "Anything back from your crime scene people?"

Let's wait for Michael," I said. "No point in repeatin' myself."

As if on cue, Michael opened the door and came in. He went straight to the chair at the head of the table as usual.

"Morning," he said as he settled onto his chair. "What news?"

"First, I haven't received any word back from my people yet, even the coroner is runnin' late. However, Pete and I did go down to the kill site last night, as you know. We met up with our man, Jack findlay, him an' Zimmerman were tailin' Mitchell. He found Zimmerman's body. He was definitely murdered, His body was dragged into an alley," I said, pausing a second to let that sink in. "His throat was cut. Thing is, the cut looked a lot like the one done on the Greshenko brother. Deep. Made with an extremely sharp blade an' by someone whose fairly strong, I'd say. Findlay pointed out a house that Mitchell apparently stopped at where he had a set-to with some woman."

"A woman?" Michael asked.

"Yeah. I'm guessin it was the Frenchwoman, Dumont. We went to the house an' went inside over the objections of the landlord. We searched her rooms an' noted that when she left, it looked like she did so in a hurry; most of her clothes were still there. We finished up an' left. I had my men go in an' do a complete rummage around."

"That it?" Phil asked.

"Not quite," I said, pulling out the papers I found and passed them to him.

"Looks like Mitchell has some explainin' to do," I said.

Phil quickly flipped through the pages then said," Mother of God. These are specifications for our latest sighting systems for the new four-inch deck guns." He passed them off to Michael.

After a cursory glance at them he said, "And you are sure that Mitchell passed these on to the Russian?"

"Who else could it be?" I asked him.

"I am only asking because as I understand it, Mitchell is an electrician not an electronics technician."

"Yeah, so?"

"So, there is no way he would have access to this level of information."

"Damn, you're right," Phil said. "That means..."

"There's someone else workin' for the Russian," I said finishing his statement.

"I think we more or less thought that would be the case," Michael said. "It is almost certain that he would have a small number of contacts. However, these papers change our strategy somewhat."

"Does that mean we pick him up?" I asked.

"As much as I would like to find this new security threat it may be time to take more direct action, so yes, it is time to make an arrest."

Just then the door opened, and Pete stepped into the room and took a seat at the table.

"Sorry I'm late," he said, "but I jus' had an interestin' conversation with one of my snitches. It seems our main suspect, Larry Mitchell, has been seen with another fella who works in the shipyard. Somethin' to do electronics, so my man sez."

"Interesting," Michael said.

"Get a name?" I asked.

"Better than that. I stopped at the station an' took a chance an' called that security fella, Allard, at the shipyard. He agreed to send the personnel file down on Jack Markham by a runner. It should be here shortly."

"Wanna bet he's our other man?" I asked, looking at Phil.

"Seems to point that way. I wonder if this Markham and Mitchell are working together?" he said.

"It's a definite possibility," I said. "I got an idea, but let's wait on the file. Speakin' of which, the Mitchell file; anythin' in it on his habits, you know, booze, gamblin', that sort of thing? I mean, I'm assumin' that you people would look at those sorts of things as possible exposure to subversion or other risks."

"We do run thorough background checks on any personnel engaged on work in any sensitive areas, of course," Michael said, a bit defensively. "However, it is possible that these two men may not have been vetted to that degree."

I gave him a questioning look.

"Not that high level, although, they would have been screened to some degree."

"I'll pull Mitchell's file as well as Markham's," Phil said. He reached for the phone that was on the table. When it was answered he instructed the listener to bring in the files.

"You have files on these men?" Pete asked.

"We have files on everyone employed by the military and the government; it's routine," he said. "And yes, Pete, before you ask, we have files on you and Robie, otherwise, you wouldn't have received your security clearance."

"Jus' askin'," Pete said, holding up a hand.

The door opened and a rating stepped inside.

"Sorry to interrupt," he said, "But there's a call for Detective Robichaud. It's from the police department."

"Transfer it to this line," Phil said.

"Yes sir. Right away." He left, closing the door behind him. A moment later another rating, this time a WAVE, knocked and come in. She was carrying two manila files. She set them on the table then quickly left.

Phil pulled the files over and started to look through them.

"Do we have any idea where to find the Russian?" Michael asked while Phil continued reading and I waited for the call to be transferred.

"No," I said. "It was jus' by chance we located the place where the woman was. It looks like he might have stayed there as well."

"So, what is your next move?"

"Not sure at the moment. Let's wait an' see what the station's got. I've been waitin' on the crime scene an' coroner's reports."

Just at that moment the phone rang. I got up and went round the table to the phone and picked it up.

"Robichaud," I said into the mouthpiece then after a few moments said, "just read it to me."

A few minutes later I told the person on the other end to put the scraps in an envelope and send them down here by squad car right away then hung up and sat back down in my chair.

"That was the crime scene report," I said. "The coroner's is still not in. As I told you earlier, I had the team go over the woman's room an' give it a thorough look. Turns out they did find a coupla things might be useful."

"Oh?" Michael said.

"They found some scraps of paper in a wastebasket. They appear to be written in French, probably from her contacts back in Quebec. There also one written in another language they couldn't decipher. I'm guessin' it might in Russian. They should be here soon."

At this point, Phil looked up from the files.

"Anythin'?" Pete asked.

"Nothing that would jump out on a preliminary inspection. There are several minor items taken on their own would not have rang any bells but looked at together...maybe."

"Such as?"

"Well, it's mostly the Markham file. It looks like he has a taste for cards and women."

"Hell, that don't mean anythin'; does it? I mean, come down to it, so do I."

"That may be so, Pete," Michael put in, "but for someone working with the level of security as he does, these vices could leave him open to being compromised."

"Compromised, you mean blackmail, right?" Michael simply nodded his head. "What is it?"

"I was jus' remembering somethin' Mike Butler told me," he said.

"Mike Butler?"

"Yeah, he's one of my snitches. Works in some 'a the clubs 'round town. When I talked to him 'bout the Russian an' Mitchell he said somethin' 'bout seein' him with a bloke he reckoned was his mate. Anyway, the other fella turns out to be Markham an', accordin' to Butler, this Markham has a bit of a reputation with some 'a the gamin' rooms. Mostly he loses an' ends up runnin' tabs with the ones runnin' the games. He said that Markham is known to go for women, usually on the younger side."

"You mean underage?" Michael asked with a disgusted look on his face.

"He didn't know but said some a them were pretty close to the line."

"That'd make him a prime target for the Russian," I said.

Michael looked at Phil and said in a slightly angry tone of voice, "Why was this not caught when he was being screened?"

"He was hired back in early nineteen-forty. The screening system we were working with at the time was not ready for what was coming. Unfortunately, it looks like Markham slipped through the system as improved methods were incorporated. He wasn't re-assessed," Phil said, looking at

Michael. "No one's fault. He just happened to arrive here looking for work at the same time as hundreds of others that were needed immediately to deal with the transitions. The good news is we know exactly where to pick him up as well as Mitchell if that is still your thinking."

"Let me consider this for the moment. I will give you my decision shortly. Thank you everyone," Michael said, standing up, then looking at Pete and me, added, "Outstanding work, especially you two."

Phil, Pete, and I stayed on a while longer discussing the information contained in Mitchell and Markham's personnel files. Besides, I wanted to see the crime scene report, especially the part where they went through the woman's room. They arrived fifteen minutes later.

"Anything interesting?" Pete asked.

"They found some partially burned scraps of paper in the stove," I said, passing them to him and Phil. "According to them, there wasn't much left, however, two or three still had writing on them, mostly letters or partially burnt letters and a number. You guys make anythin' out what there?"

"Pretty hard," Pete said, scrutinizing a scrap. This one has the letters, I see a 'He' then a 't' I think then a 'r'."

"Same here," Phil said. "This one might be referring to someplace in Dartmouth, I think."

"Why do think that" I asked.

"I recognized some of the letters. I think it's a street down by the ferry on the Dartmouth side. Also, I think this might have been written in French. There's an accent over one of the letters."

"Funny you say that," Pete said. "This one looks like it's also written in a foreign language, though I got no idea what one." He passed it to me.

"I think it's Russian," I said. "I seen it before, it's called Cyrillic or somethin' like that."

"Makes sense it'd be there since we know they're traveling together," Phil said. "Listen, can you leave this stuff with me. I can have our lab people go through it, maybe they'll find more. No slight to your people, of course, it's just we have more resources to work with."

"No offense taken an', yeah, let's see what they can come up with, the more heads the better. If that's it for now, Pete and me will head out. There's somethin' I wanna look into. Call me if Michael makes a decision on pickin' up the Russian."

"Will do," Phil said, getting up as well. "Later."

* * *

Wallace was sitting at his usual place: the kitchen table, when suddenly he sensed someone standing behind him. He cautiously turned in his seat. Kelly Johns loomed over him.

He stood over six foot and looked to weigh in at about two-fifty. He had long black hair with two braided lengths hanging down his front. He was clean shaven; Indians didn't seem to be able to grow breads, though the skin was pock marked. His eyes were like two black coals set in his face under heavy brows. He wore a soiled black overcoat, tied around the middle with a length of quarter inch rope.

"Jesus Christ," Wallace yelled. "Ya scared the livin' shit outta me. How da hell ya get I here?"

"I hear you lookin' for me," Johns said in a calm even voice. "Here I am."

"Yeah...here ya are. Right. I need ya to do a job for me."

Johns just stood there, quietly...waiting.

"I need someone taken out, ya get what I'm sayin'?"

"Who?"

"I'll let ya know."

"How much?"

"A hunnerd bucks."

"Two," Johns said.

"What! Ya want two hunnerd? How come?" Wallace asked.

"Times tough."

"Okay. Deal," he said. "When can you do da job?"

"When do ya need it done?"

"Right away, that gonna be a problem?"

"No. You pay now."

"Not a chance," Wallace said, taking out his wallet and pulling out two ten-dollar banknotes. He knew if he gave that much money to the Indian, he would be passed out drunk before dark. "Here's twenty. The rest when da job's done. Take it or leave it."

Johns grabbed the bills and stuffed them in his coat pocket.

Wallace then gave him a full description of Petrov, telling him to hook up with Roode who would set him up with the target. When he finished, Johns turned and left as quietly as he came.

"Sampson!" he yelled. "Git yer arse in 'ere."

A few moments later Joe Sampson stepped into the kitchen.

"Yeah? Whaddya want," he said. "I was busy in da basement."

Kelly Johns was jus' 'ere. Walks in cool as ya please. Damn near scared the life outta me."

"Yeah?"

"Yeah. Da son of a bitch ain't fuckin' human. I didn't 'ere a Goddamn thing. Next I knows he's standin' dere behind me."

"Jesus. So? Did ya work it out with'im?"

"Yeah. He's gonna do it. Tole 'im to hook up with Roode next time da Russian calls."

"So you're goin' through with it then?"

"No choice. Things is getting' outta hand. He's killin' people, fer Chrissake, an' dat sorta shit we don't need."

"Why don't we jus' cut 'im loose?"

"Cain't. 'E sez we're in an' no way out til 'e's done."

Jesus."

"No shit."

"Now what?'

"Wait fer 'im ta call den get Roode to call Johns."

"Better hope Johns is up to it or we're next."

Wallace eyed his right-hand man, noting that he looked nervous.

"We still got the hardware in da house?"

"Yeah, in da basement, why?" Sampson asked.

"Better fish it out. Git me my Webley an' sum spare rounds. Pick one fer yerself."

"Jesus," he said for the second time as he turned around and headed for the basement.

Chapter Thirteen

We finished up our meeting shortly after the files from the station arrived. Pete and I headed back to Church Street to see the landlord at the house where the Dumont woman stayed. Something about the man rubbed me the wrong way. It wasn't just his attitude towards us; it was something else.

"What's put a bee in your bonnet 'bout this guy?" Pete asked.

"Don't rightly know exactly," I said as we drove up South Street towards Queen Street. "Jus' call it a cop feelin'."

"You think he knows somethin' or maybe has somethin'?"

"That's what I wanna check out."

I turned onto Queen then headed for Morris Street where I turned right onto Church. It was one way heading back to South Street. I pulled the car to the curb across from the house and we got out. Pete banged on the door and after a several moments the landlord opened up.

He looked better in the daylight; dressed in work pants, a plaid shirt and work shoes. He had shaved and his hair was combed straight back. In the daylight he looked younger compared to what I saw last night; about early forties, I guessed.

"Oh," he said. "You're back then. I thought you people got everything you wanted last night."

"We got some more questions we wanna ask you," I said. "Can we come in?"

"Yeah, I 'spose so." He stepped aside and we walked into the foyer. "In there."

He pointed to a small sitting room off to the right.

"Sit if you want. I got the kettle on if you want tea."

"We're good," I said. Thanks. My name is Robichaud an' this is Detective Duncan. You are?"

"Oliver Niven."

"This place yours?"

"That's right. Used to belong to my parents. They retired a while back and sold it to me. Why?"

"Jus' background for our report," I said.

His demeanor definitely had improved from last night. I was beginning to feel less ill-disposed toward him.

"So? Whaddya want ask me about?"

"How long has the Frenchwoman been livin' here?" I asked. Pete had his notebook out, as usual.

"'Bout a month and a half."

"An' the fella, he been livin' here to?"

"Yeah, off and on," he said.

"What's that mean, on an' off? Did he live here or not?'

"I would say yeah, most of the time. He was out a lot."

"Any other renters?" Pete asked.

"One. He rents a room up in the attic I converted over. His name is Robertson. Works as a night watchman in one of the department stores downtown."

"How did you know the man with Dumont was foreigner? I asked.

"Dumont? Who the hell is this Dumont?" Niven asked.

"The woman."

"That wasn't the name she used. Called herself Mombourquette. Said she was up from Yarmouth looking for work. As for the man, I knew wasn't from here; his accent, it didn't sound like any I heard before."

"Did you ever pick up on any conversations they might've had?"

"Not really. They kept themselves to themselves and I don't usually go around listening in on other people's conversations." I noted something in the tone of voice he used when he said this. I stared at him for a moment, waiting.

"However," he said.

Here it comes, I thought.

"However, I walked in on them about a week ago in the kitchen and overheard the woman say something about going to see someone in the west end."

"Happen to hear where?" Pete asked.

"Someplace on Edinburgh Street."

"That's it?" I asked. "No address or name?"

He shook his head, then, "Oh, wait a sec. I think I heard her say Piaf, or something like that. I remember because it sounded so odd."

"Well, that about does it for now, thanks for your help." I offered him my hand. "We'll find our way out."

"By the way, when can I rent that room out again. I was told it was part of a criminal investigation and no one was to go inside."

"I'll see what I can do."

As we walked across the street to the car, Pete said, "So, whaddya think?"

"Never go with your gut feelin' alone," I said. "I read the man wrong last night. Let's leave it at that. Now we head back to the station. I wanna chase down this person Piaf."

When I got back to the station, I found the coroner's report waiting for me on my desk and a note to see Morrison. I knew what the boss wanted but took a minute to review the report.

According to the M.E., Zimmerman died from a massive penetrating cut to the throat which would have caused a massive shock to his heart, resulting in an instant death. He also bled out due to the severing of the carotid arteries in his neck. He also surmised that the weapon had to be extremely sharp and wielded by a very strong man.

He estimated that the blade had to be at least eight inches long by two inches in width, noting that he could not liken it to any blades he was familiar with. Lastly, he noted that the cut was almost identical to the one that killed Greshenko.

Basically, the report only confirmed what I already guessed. I put the report down then headed upstairs to see Morrison. Before going, I told Pete to start looking into the name Niven gave us.

I went into his office and took my usual seat in front of his desk. He set his pen down and sat back in his chair.

"Mornin'," I said.

"What's the latest?" he said in his usual direct manner.

We have worked together a long time, so I was familiar with his directness and did not take offense. We came to a comfortable understanding about each other a long time ago.

"Parks is considerin' issuing the okay to pick up the Russian."

"Finally. What changed his mind?"

"The death of Zimmerman, I think. He was one of his men."

"What have you learned in that regard?"

I gave him a detailed account of what happened last night, including Findlay's report.

"Me an' Pete went inside an' searched the room rented by the Frenchwoman that's when I found some documents stuffed in the sofa. They were technical drawings and information that, accordin' to Phil, were to do with some new weapon system. Anyway, it confirms the connection between Mitchell an' someone else named Markham, an' the Russian agent."

"You gave the documents to them I assume," he said.

"Yeah, figured they'd want them back under lock an' key, besides, they had no direct relevance to my investigation. They will be used as evidence when they arrest Mitchell and Markham."

"Anything else?"

"I had a talk with the landlord, his name is Oliver Niven. All he could tell us was he thought he heard them leave in a hurry. I had a feelin' about the landlord, so me an' Pete went back to talk to him this mornin'. Turns out he overheard the pair of them talkin' a while back, an' thought he heard her mention Edinburgh Street an' a name, Piaf."

"Piaf?" Morrison said. "Odd name."

"Yeah. It's French, but not one you'd normally find here in the Maritimes. I'm guessin' it's a European name."

"You think it might mean something?"

195

"Don't know," I said. "Can't think of a reason why it should. Takin' a wild guess, I'd reckon they came over before the war started or before the Germans invaded France. What I'm more curious about is what is the connection this person has to her?"

"I assume you're looking into that?"

"Jus' as soon as I finish up here."

"Good. Don't let me keep you," he said, picking up his pen.

The meeting was over.

"Any luck?" I asked Pete when I entered the squad room, heading for his desk.

"Still checkin'," he said, looking up at me. "Nothin' in the phone directory. I got a call in to someone I know works at the phone company to see if there's number that isn't listed. How'd it go upstairs?"

"Usual. Keep goin' an' keep in touch."

"So? Now what?"

"What's the latest on findin' Kelly Johns?'

"Dunno. Hey, George," he called over to one of the detectives in the room with us.

"Yeah?" George Kendricks answered, looking over at us.

"You got anythin' on Kelly Johns yet?"

It was him and his partner, Jack Rawlins, that told us about Wallace wanting to see Johns.

"Nothin' yet. Ya know he don't have a fixed address an' he's barred from most a the drinking spots. We're lookin' inta a few of the flops we know he uses."

"Okay, thanks. Let us know right away when you get somethin'," Pete said.

Yeah, will do."

"Right," I said. "There's gotta be somethin' we missed back there at the woman's place."

"Like what? I mean, me an' you went through the place then crime scene fellas did the same. If we missed somethin' I sure as hell don't know what it could'a been."

"Yeah. Still...it's a pain in the ass. The thing that's nippin' at me is how fast they got away. Accordin' to Findlay's report the total time between him followin' Mitchell an' Zimmerman getting' killed couldn't been more than ten minutes, maybe a few minutes more.'

"Yeah, I s'pose so?"

"Didn't strike you as odd that when we searched her rooms there wasn't much left there?"

"Whaddya mean?"

"Clothes, shoes, her toiletries, crap like that."

"Damn, you're right, now you mention it. That means she, or them, were travelin' light."

"Or were ready to flee at a moment's notice," I said. "Do you remember askin' Niven if he remembered her havin' any luggage when she moved in?"

"Shit, no. You?" he asked.

"No," I said, shaking my head.

We spent the next half hour catching up on outstanding cases before a call from Roode came through to me.

"Whaddya got?" I asked when I picked up the phone.

"Da boss jus' tole me to call Johns if da Russki calls me," he said.

"He say why?"

"Nope. Jus' t'aught ya'd wanna know."

"Okay. Call me when you get a call."

"Yeah, sure t'ing."

I hung up the phone.

Got somethin'?" Pete asked, looking over at me.

"Don't know," I said. "That was Roode. He said that Wallace told him to contact Johns if the Russian calls him to pick him up."

"Now what the hell you think that means?"

"No good, I'm thinkin'," I said with a shrug. "I can only think of two possibilities. One. The Russian needs someone for a job, or, two, he's gonna use Johns to take out the Russian."

"Jesus. That's a pretty big leap in thinkin'. I can see the first possibility, but how did you reckon on the second?"

"I know it's a wild guess," I said. "But, consider what we know about Wallace."

"Okay," Pete said.

"He's a third-rate villain; no real connections to the hard boys, right? So, suddenly he has a chance to play in the big leagues with the Russian. But we know he's never been involved in anythin' worse than strong armin' people for collections. Now he finds himself into somethin' where people are gettin' killed."

"Yeah, I see that. He's gotta be wettin' himself knowin' he'd be tied into the murders."

"Uh-huh," I said. "Plus, we know that the Russian doesn't operate by the same rules as we do an' likely made it clear to him that there wasn't any way out."

"Makes sense. This guy is used to puttin' the fear of God into people. So, you think maybe the best road for him to get out this business is to knock off the Russian. Pretty risky, especially for Wallace."

"Hmmm. Like I said, it's a wild thought."

After a brief moment, Pete said, "If you're right, an' let's hope you're not, this could end up with a lot more bodies. You gonna run this by Phil?"

"Yeah, I thought I would. After all, it concerns his people too."

When I arrived at Headquarters, Phil met me in the canteen in the basement.

"Looks like Michael's made his decision," he said, once we were seated at a corner table.

"Yeah?," I said. "And...?"

"We're picking them up. The whole lot of them. Mitchell. Markham. The Russian and the woman. You can bring in Wallace and his gang. I've already dispatched a couple of my men to the shipyard to get Markham and two more for Mitchell."

"What about Dumont an' Petrov? They're gone, remember?

"Yeah, I know," he said. "I'm counting on you and Pete finding them."

"Thought you might."

"I got a team standing by to go once you locate them. How's that going, by the way?"

"We're followin' up on a couple of possible leads. The landlord told us he overheard them talkin' once an' thought he heard the woman mention Edinburgh Street. We're also lookin' into somethin' we might've pick up from those fragments of burnt paper."

"Great. Call me once you have something, anything that might lead us to them, and I'll set the operation in motion right away."

"What's the plan if we do catch them?" I asked. "You know I still want him for at least two murders?"

"First thing is to catch. Then once that's done, we put them in custody while we try and figure out how to go forward. As you know, this is a tricky situation. Petrov is not officially an enemy agent, but an ally. Admittedly he is stealing secrets but..."

"I get that, but I'm jus' a cop an' he's broken our laws here. He has to be made accountable for that, at least that's what the mayor and' Crown Prosecutor will say. They're gonna want their pound of flesh and, for that matter, so do I."

"I do sympathize with you, Robie. I'm a cop as well and I wouldn't like to see a murderer walk free. Thing is. Petrov is guilty of stealing our secret and of committing murder. Plus, he is a foreign national of a country that is an ally in our fight against Hitler. It's possible he could walk, claiming diplomatic immunity."

"Horse shit," I said. "If I have the chance, the bastard will cool his heels in my jail."

"Actually, you know, that might not be a bad idea," Phil said.

Huh?"

"Think about it. If we take him into custody, his government would be all over Ottawa for his release but, if he were arrested and charged under our civil law for a capital crime...?

"They'd have jurisdiction," I said, finishing his thought.

"It's thin, I admit, but it would throw a wrench in any attempt by the delegation in Ottawa to grab him."

"Not to worry," I said, "once he's in my custody, I'll put him under lock and key at the station an' officially charged before the dust settles. I better get outta here. I need to fill Morrison in so he can get things started with the mayor an' the Crown."

"I hoped you'd say that. By the way, what brought you in? I was going to call but you beat to it."

I filled him in on Roode's call and Kelly Johns. Then I ran my thinking by him as to what I thought Wallace might be up to.

"Sounds like Michael's decision came at the right time, otherwise there might have been more unnecessary killings."

"No kiddin'. Wallace has no idea the can of worms he's about to open if he is plannin' to take out the Russian. I'll send a couple of squad cars down to his place an' make the arrests."

"Good luck."

"Thanks."

When I got back to the station, I saw Pete was busy lookin' through some of the bits of paper we picked up from Church Street. He was waiting for his contact at the phone company lookin' to see if there were any Piaf's listed to call back.

"Nothin' yet?" I asked when I arrived.

"No," he said, looking up at me. "Problem is, the phone company's pretty touchy 'bout givin' out information without warrants. I didn't think we had enough to go to the Crown to get one. How'd it go downtown?"

"Michael's decided to round the whole lotta them up, includin' the Russian, if we can find him," I said.

"Finally."

"Phil's sent his people out to pick up Mitchell an' Markham as we speak. Look, I gotta go upstairs. While I do that, you set up the raid on Wallace's place an' make sure you take Roode in as well. No point in settin' him up as a snitch. Send Rawlins or Kendricks with the uniforms."

"My pleasure. By the way, what are we chargin' him with?"

"Let's really stick it to him; accessory to murder an' sellin' secret documents. That'll put the frighteners on the bastard."

I turned and headed for the stairs with sound of Pete's laughter behind me.

Ten minutes later, I finished my report to Morrison, adding, "We gotta find him first, then when we do, we'll arrest him an' lock him up downstairs. Hopefully, the mayor and Crown will come up with somethin' to let us keep him."

"Then what?" he asked, looking across at me. "If we can't, they get to keep him?"

"Not exactly. I was thinkin' if the Crown can submit the formal charges to the court fast enough then the matter would be in the system, right?"

I filled him in on my talk with Phil.

"I knew there was a reason I liked that guy," he said, smiling. "So now what?"

"Hopefully, Phil can convince Michael of our plan. If he does, then there's a good chance we'll be able to try the son of a bitch."

"The important thing is to get him off the street an' outta our hair," he said leaning forward. "What happens after that, well..." He left the question hang there.

"You know the worse that'd happen is the possibility the bastard'll walk?"

He shrugged.

"I don't like it any more than you, Robie, but this case is way over our heads."

"Yeah," he said sourly, "tell that to Zimmerman's family."

I watched him lower his gaze. He was a good man and stood for something he believed in, justice. I felt somewhere deep inside that even though the years had beaten me down some, I understood.

Chapter Fourteen

Jack Markham was working on a piece of electronic equipment with two other technicians when he saw a couple of men in overcoats and hats through the window of the work room walk down the hall. Something about their look gave him pause; security men, he thought. What could that mean? he wondered.

Ten minutes later, Luc Allard and the two men stepped into the room and approached his worktable.

"Jack Markham," one of the men said. "I am Constable Lewis with Naval Intelligence. Under the National Defense Act we are placing you under arrest for espionage. Turn around."

The other man stepped to him and grabbed his arm, turning him around then he felt the cold metal of the shackles being clasped around his wrist.

"I...I don't know what you mean...what espionage?" he started to protest. The two men said nothing. "I know my rights. You can't just take me away. I want a lawyer."

The two technicians he was working with moved away from the table to stand with Allard by the wall.

Markham was led out of the room, a man on either side holding his elbows, and down the hall to a waiting car that would deliver him to Naval Headquarters.

Little did he know that an exact same scene was being played out down in the dockyard.

Mitchell and Markham found themselves sitting, manacled, in separate rooms at Naval Headquarters with only an armed shore patrolman standing guard.

Phil entered the room with Mitchell and sat down across from him. He had a file and a notepad in his hand which he set down in front of him and opened it.

"You are in very serious trouble," he said when he looked up at Mitchell. "Let me be crystal clear with you. We know that you have been passing secret information to a Russian agent. Normally that would mean, if convicted, you would hang, but since this agent is from a government that is currently an ally and not an enemy, you will be imprisoned for the rest of your life. Do you understand what I'm telling you?"

Mitchell nodded.

"Right. Let's start then. Tell me everything you know about this agent, starting with how he made contact with you."

An hour later, Phil had everything he needed to know as Mitchell spilled his guts in the hope that his cooperation would get him a break.

"Very good," Phil said. "Now. Tell me about Jack Markham."

"You know about Jack?" Mitchell said, looking surprised. "Christ."

"He isn't going to help you. Jack Markham?"

Mitchell thought for a moment. He had no idea what the authorities already knew and he did not like ratting out a friend but...

"Whaddya want to know?"

"Let's start with how he got connected to the Russian?"

"I sort'a introduced them."

"Why would you do that and what made you think of him?"

"Me an' Jack met a while back shortly after he came here from Toronto. We became drinkin' buddies, see. Anyway, I soon learned he had a taste for women an' gambling an' wanted me to get him into a game somewhere. It didn't take him long to make his own contacts. Later, I heard from some people who know we're friends that he's into a coupla the guys who run the games," Mitchell said, pausing for a moment.

"Yeah, then what?" Phil asked.

"One night, the Russian asked if I knew anyone else who he could contact. That's when I thought of Jack. I knew he needed the money an' he worked in a place with better information than I did. So, I told him I knew he needed cash an' that I knew someone who could help him out."

"And?"

"An' that's it. I put them together an' left them to make their deal."

"Okay. What about this woman, Celeste Dumont? Who is she and what's her connection in all this?"

"Jesus," Mitchell swore, "what the hell don't you know?"

"Never mind that, just believe we know so don't even try and protect her."

"Protect her! You gotta be kiddin'. I hope you nail the bitch's ass to the wall."

"So?"

"All I know 'bout her is she's from Quebec an' she's hooked up with the Russian."

"How do mean, hooked up?" Phil asked.

"You know, hooked up." He made a slightly obscene motion. "I think she also looks for pigeons like me the Russian can buy."

"How does she find people like you?"

"She works down at the Lantern. I go there a lot to eat. She chatted me up an', well, one thing led to another an'..." He left the idea hang there for a moment.

"And that's how you got in with them?"

"Yeah, after 'a coupla dates she introduces me to the Russian an' we started hangin' out' you know, boozin', havin' a good time. Then one night he asks me if I'd be interested in picking some extra money. Celeste has expensive tastes an' I don't make so much to keep up with her. So, I say sure, why not."

"It didn't occur to you that you were committing treason?"

"Treason?" he said, with a hint of panic in his voice. "What the hell do you mean, treason?"

"You sold secret information to a foreign national. That's treason."

"But he's an ally, right? He wasn't an enemy agent, for Chrissake."

"That doesn't matter," Phil said. "You had no authority to take whatever information you did, and it was definitely illegal to sell it."

"Oh my God," he whined. What'll happen to me?"

"Up to me, I scc swing, but it isn't up to me. So, you will be placed before the courts and they'll decide."

"God help me."

"If you're lucky."

Phil stood up and gathered the file and notepad, then, ordered the guard that Mitchell done and to take him to the secure holding area in the basement.

Out in the hall he saw Michael come towards him.

"I was just coming down to see you," Phil said.

"Come inside then," Parks said as they entered his office.

"I heard you have picked up Mitchell and Markham?" Parks said as they both sat down.

"I just finished my initial interrogation of Mitchell," Phil said, nodding. "Markham's next. He's in the other interrogation room under guard."

"Anything enlightening come to light?"

"Nothing shattering, however, Mitchell account seems to cover a lot of what we were guessing. I made notes and will have a written report on your desk by end of day. I was actually on my way to interrogate Markham when I saw coming down the hall."

"Good. Mind if I sit in?"

"Not all. Two is always better than one in these situations, besides, seeing you might instill a sense of fear. You know, suggesting that his fate could be in the hands of military justice and not civilian."

"You do have a nasty mind," Parks said with a wry smile. "Shall go and scare the bastard."

They both stood and headed for the interrogation room and Jack Markham.

Jack Markham sat manacled on the hard wooden chair, looking around the stark, windowless room. The only other person in there was the armed shore patrolman who stood behind him.

"Hey," he said, turning his head slightly to the right. "What's the chance of getting' a cigarette?"

All he got by way of an answer was silence.

"Yeah. To hell with you."

The door opened and Phil and Michael entered the room. The sailor came to attention.

"That's okay, sailor," Phil said to the guard. "You can wait outside. Have a smoke if you want."

"Sir."

The two men pulled chairs over and sat down.

"About Goddamn time," Markham snapped. "When am I gonna see my solicitor?"

"Solicitor?" Phil said, evenly. "What makes you think you are entitled to a solicitor?"

"I know my rights. You can't arrest me without allowing me to council."

"But, dear boy," Parks said. "You are not under arrest."

"Not under...," Markham said, suspiciously. "then get these off of me and let me go."

"Sorry. No can do."

"But...?"

"I did say you were not under arrest, true, however, you are being detained under the War Act on the charge of espionage, and that is under the jurisdiction of Military Intelligence. Not the civilian authorities."

"What!"

"Now let's begin. The first thing we want to know is…"

"Wait. Wait a Goddamn minute," Markham said, raising his voice slightly. "Whaddya mean espionage? I'm no traitor."

"You stole military secrets and passed them to a foreign agent," Phil said. "That's espionage."

"Okay, I admit I took some documents and, yes, I passed them on to a foreigner, but he wasn't an enemy agent, for Chrissake. He said he was Russian and they're our allies, right? He said his country was only interested in the information to help them defend themselves. How the hell is that espionage?"

"Let's not get off on the wrong foot here. You didn't do this out of any sense of mutual cooperation with a supposed ally. You did this for money. Plain and simple. You see, we know about your gambling debts and other, um, expensive interests. Understand?"

Markham slumped in his seat. He knew he was done for and in no position to protest.

"So, back to my question, who else is involved with taking documents?"

"And I want to know exactly how many and which documents you took?" Michael added.

"I... I don't know anyone else. I did it on my own."

"And the documents? What did you take and how many?"

He was beaten and knew it. He leaned forward and started to list what he took, detailing how he got into the secure files and got them out of the shipyard. When he finished a half hour later, Michael ordered the guard to take him to the basement and put him in the cell with Mitchell.

"It could've been worse," Phil said. "A whole lot worse."

"There is that," Michael answered as they walked down the hall.

"Now what? We can't keep them here?"

"I'll make arrangements to transfer them over to the army up at the Citadel. Then I'll contact Ottawa and get their instructions. What's the latest from Robie and his efforts to find the Russian?"

"He was here earlier. Looks like they may have got a break and located another possible location where Petrov and the woman may have gone. I believe they are planning on looking into it."

"Let's hope he is successful," Michael said when they reached the door to his office. "I want this business over and done as quickly as possible. There have been far too many deaths and I do not want to see any more. Oh, on that subject, what progress are you making concerning Zimmerman's family?"

"I have been in touch with them personally and I am sending an official letter of commendation to our headquarters with a recommendation that they see to his family's financial security."

"Excellent. Well, keep me updated on Robie's progress," he said, opening the door. "And Phil, good work back there."

"Thanks." He continued on down the hall to his office.

* * *

Henry Wallace was sitting in his den listening to the radio with a glass of rum in hand. He always sat at the radio this time of day to listen to his favorite performer, Don Messer. Usually, his men knew not to disturb him at these times.

"Hey boss," Joe Sampson said as he stepped into the room.

"I know, I know," Sampson said, "we ain't to bother bother ya when yer listenin' to da radio, but it's da Russian on da phone."

"Jesus Christ," Wallace swore as he lifted himself off his chair. "Outta da way."

He stormed past Sampson to the phone out in the foyer.

"Yeah?" he snapped when he picked up the earpiece.

"Need driver," Petrov said, ignoring Wallace's tone.

"When an' where?'

214

"Now." He then told him where he would be waiting.

"Half an hour," Wallace said then hung up. It happened that Roode was already there at the house. So, it was easy to set it up. He gave Roode his instructions then dialed the number Johns had given him where he could be reached.

"It's me. You ready to do dat job we talked about?"

"Yes," Johns said.

"Where are ya?"

"Where's this man you want gone?"

"He'll be at the corner of Queen and Tobin Streets in a half hour near the church, why?"

"I will call when job done." Then the line went dead.

He had already given Johns a pretty good description of the Russian, so he was sure he'd pick him out. He turned to Roode and told him to take off for the location he gave Johns, just in case something went wrong. He was to pick up the Russian if he was still alive and do whatever he said then call back to tell him.

Roode nodded and headed for the door.

"Okay," Roode said, trying to think where the closest telephone was located so he could call Robichaud; he couldn't go directly to the police station because he might be seen. He drove a few blocks away to a drugstore he knew was in the area. If he remembered right, they had a payphone.

He went inside and found the phone booth in the back. Unfortunately, Robichaud was not in, and he decided not to leave a message. He hung up and returned to the car.

Roode drove down to Barrington Street then headed for the south end. He planned to take Tobin Street up to Queen. He pulled the car over about six houses down from the church and shut the motor off. Sitting there in the dark, he had a clear view of the upper end of the street, including the corner of the church. Ten minutes later, he spotted the Russian. He had a woman with him.

Suddenly he saw a shadowy figure emerge from out of the shadows, crouching slightly with his arm held out in front of him. Then he heard a faint scream as the woman jumped out of the way.

He watched as the big Russian spun around just as Johns lunged with his knife. The Russian deflected the thrust and countered with his fist into Johns' throat, staggering him. He watched in horror as the Russian grabbed Johns by the throat as he was carried forward with the momentum of his thrust, then in a violent pull, he ripped the soft part under his chin out.

It was all Roode could do not to empty his guts in the car.

Then, through bleary eyes he saw the Russian grab the woman and move back into the shadows. A moment later he reappeared and pulled Johns' dead body into the shadowed area as well.

It took him several minutes to regain some degree of composure before he started the car up and drove to the corner. He left the lights off, not wanting to see the blood that would be there. When he stopped the two people rushed out of the shadows and got in the back of the car.

"Drive," the Russian snapped, sounding calm, controlled.

Roode could tell that he was completely impassive to what he just did; ripping a man's throat out was nothing more to him than swatting a fly.

"Where ya wanna go?' he asked, trying to keep the fear out of his voice.

"Edinburgh Street," the woman said, sounding shaky.

"You know this street?" the Russian asked.

"Yeah," Roode said, shifting into third and headed for South where he would turn left and head for Robie Street.

"Who do think that man was?" the woman asked.

"Don't know," Petrov answered. "Maybe a thief."

"Your hand. It is full of blood. Here." She opened her handbag and pulled out a white handkerchief and handed it to him. He took it and started to wipe his hand.

They were on Robie Street when the Russian said, "Slow down. You go to fast. Do not get stopped."

Roode did not see he was in fact speeding, he was so upset by what he witnessed.

"Huh?," he said, looking at the speedometer. "Oh, yeah, sure, sorry 'bout dat."

He eased off the accelerator and the car's speed dropped down.

They finally arrived at the destination.

"You want me to stay?" Roode asked out his window after the two got out.

"No. Go. Tell Wallace I will call if I need you again."

'He don't hafta tell me twice,' Roode thought as he pulled away from the curb and sped away.

"What's the matter, *Cheri*?" Dumont asked, looking at him as watched the car drive off.

"Something not right."

"What?"

"Not sure. Enough. Let us go inside."

At that exact moment, in another part of the city, Detective Rawlins and six uniformed officers were crashing into Henry Wallace's house with guns drawn.

Chapter Fifteen

It was late in the afternoon, and we were back at the station when the call from Phil came in. He managed to get inside the phone company's records and managed to find the information on Piaf. His full name was Marcel Piaf, formally from Trois Rivieres, Quebec. Their records showed that he arrived here in thirty-eight and ordered a phone installation with an unlisted number. According to Phil, Piaf supposedly lived alone.

"The address is one-twenty-three Edinburgh Street," Phil said. "You need any of my people to go with you?"

"No. We can handle it, thanks anyway. I'll call you when we're done," I said.

"Good luck."

"Got it," I called out to Pete.

He looked up from the file he was reading and said, "Got what?"

"Piaf's address. Phil came through. Grab your hat and coat. We're goin' to pay Mr. Piaf a visit. Oh, make sure your gun is ready...jus' in case."

We drove down Windsor Street, approaching the top of Edinburgh Street which was across from the Forum. I drove slowly past the row of houses looking for one-twenty-three. Then I spotted it.

It was a white single story wooden house with a small front lawn and a set of steps leading up to the front door.

"Car in the drive," Pete said as he looked out window. "Left side of the house near the back. Think they're in there?"

"That'd be my guess."

"How do you wanna do this?"

I pulled the car to the curb four doors down past the house. Looking back over my shoulder through the rear window, I said, "I don't think I want to jus' walk up to the front door. If they are in there the last thing I want is a shootout."

"I agree," Pete said. "So, what then?"

"I reckon if they see us comin' they'll make a run for the car. Let's not approach the house together. You go first. Head for the driveway. I'll make for the door an' you can cover me. Okay?"

He nodded and grabbed the door handle.

"Let's go."

Inside the house, Petrov was pacing the floor in the living room. Celeste was in the kitchen with Piaf. He suddenly stopped and went to the front window, pulling back the curtain slightly. A moment later he saw the black sedan slowly drive past with two men inside. He could see both were eyeing the house.

"Celeste," he yelled.

When she came rushing into the room, he was already moving toward her.

"We must go," he said, coolly.

"What?" she said.

"They found us."

"How?"

"Not important. Quick. Get coat."

Marcel Piaf stepped in behind her, almost colliding with her as she headed out of the room.

"What's happened?" he asked.

"Police," Dumont said. "Is there a way to drive out of here besides the front?"

"Yes. The backyard. Go through the shrubbery to the next street."

"Good. I am sorry for this."

"Don't worry about it. I haven't done anything wrong they can charge me with. Just get out of here."

I approached the front of the house as Pete took up his position in the driveway. As I walked past the window, I just caught a glimpse of three people moving around very quickly. I realized that I must have been seen, and they were about to make a run for it. I looked back at Pete and signaled for him to head to the back of the house. I dashed for the driveway.

As I neared the corner of the house, I heard Pete call out for them stop. I pulled my gun and looked around the corner just in time to see all hell break loose.

Pete was standing about twenty feet away from the Russian and woman with his gun in hand leveled at them. I saw the pair stop and then the Russian spun around, dropping to his knee. He had his weapon out and fired as soon as he had Pete in his sights. It was a single shot that caught him in the upper chest just below his shoulder. The impact spun him around as he fell to the ground.

I did not hesitate as the Russian shifted to take his next shot at me. Squeezing the trigger, I fired two shots in rapid succession; the first hit him in the stomach while the second found its mark in his neck. He managed to get a shot off at the same time but the round whistled past my ear, hitting the wooden house behind me.

The entire scene played out in less than ten seconds but felt much longer.

I dashed over to where Pete lay in a low snowbank, all the while keeping my pistol aimed at the fallen Russian and woman, who was now lying prone across his chest sobbing.

Bending down, I quickly placed my finger against Pete's neck to check for a pulse. Luckily, I found one. A moment later, I heard a siren in the distance. Someone in one of the houses must have called it in after hearing the guns shots.

The first squad car came to stop a few minutes later near where I was still kneeling next to Pete. The officer who was driving was half-way out of the car when I yelled, "Call for an ambulance. NOW."

His partner was already out and moving around the car with his weapon out.

"Go over there an' check them out," I ordered. I suddenly realized that I was still holding my gun leveled at the woman. "Make sure the bastard's dead an' cuff the woman." I slowly lowered my gun as I watched the officer cautiously approach them.

"Is he dead?" I called out.

"Yeah," he yelled back. "What a Goddamn mess. Looks like you blew his whole throat out."

"Never mind that. Hook up the woman an' put her in your car. Then go in there an' place the man inside under arrest," I said, pointing to the Piaf house.

"The ambulance is on the way," The driver said as got out of the car. "Should be here in about five minutes. How's Pete doin'?"

"It's not good, but he's still alive," I said, looking up at him. Then I recognized him. He was one of our senior officers and had worked with Pete for a while before the war. It explained the informality of using his Christen name.

Ten minutes later there were two more squad cars and the ambulance on scene. By now, the Dumont woman and Piaf were on the way down to the station. I ordered one of the squad cars to stay here and secure the house then climbed inside the ambulance behind the attendants as they pushed the gurney in.

Later, I sat in the emergency room waiting are with Aggie, Pete's wife, and their son, who sat on his mother's lap looking around at the strange surroundings. Aggie sat calmly, holding the boy close to her chest, but I could see the strain of worry on her face.

I also called Louise to come down and sit with her. She and Aggie had become good friends over these last few years.

"Coffee?" I asked, looking at her.

"Huh?," she said, startled. "Coffee? Uh. no...thanks, uh, maybe a cup of tea."

"No problem. Sit there and I'll go get it. Lou?" I asked my wife as I stood up.

"Yes, tea," Louise said. "Thanks, dear."

It was almost half an hour before the doctor came down the hall. He was still wearing his greens and surgical cap. Aggie jumped up as soon as she saw him, setting her son down at her side. Louise rose with her. I was already up.

"Mrs. Duncan?" the doctor said, looking at the two women.

Aggie took a short step forward. "Yes? Is my husband...?"

"He's out of immediate danger," the doctor said, moving to her and taking her arm sat her down, taking the chair beside her. "The bullet did not hit or damage any vital organs, however, it did damage his shoulder and surrounding muscles. In time he will recover, but with a loss of strength and some mobility in that shoulder."

"But he's okay?" she asked, her voice filled with worry.

"Yes, other than what I just told you, he'll be fine in time."

"Can I see him?"

"Not quite yet. They are taking him down to recovery at the moment and he is still under the effects of the anesthetic."

"When...?"

"Once we are sure he is stabilized and wakes up, he will be taken upstairs to a room on one of the wards. I will send a nurse down to talk with you. She will tell you everything you need to know." He stood up and started to walk away back down the hall. Louise was still holding her friend while I followed the doctor.

"Thanks Doctor," I said when I stepped up beside him. "He is gonna be okay, right?"

"Yes," he said. "In time, Uh, you are?"

"Oh, sorry. Detective Robichaud. He's my partner and friend."

"I see. Sorry."

"Will he be able to continue workin' as a cop?"

"That will up to him and how well he responds to the recovery treatment."

"He's a strong man. He'll do whatever it takes. By the way, I hafta ask, do you still have the bullet you took out of him?"

"Yes, although there was not much left."

"I don't understand."

"It is one I have not seen before. It looks like it was designed to splinter on impact, causing more damage than a regular one."

"I heard of those," I said. "Soft tipped; usually called, dum-dums. Commonly used over there by the military, especially the by the Americans."

"Over there?" he asked.

"Yeah, accordin' to what we've been told, they're used in Europe by some of the spy agencies."

"Good God."

"I don't think that's the one you otta be callin' out.

"Hm, you are right of course. Well, this is where I must leave you. Good luck with your friend."

"Thanks," I said, shaking his hand. "For everythin'. An' don't forget to send the remains of the bullet to me at the station."

I headed back to the women. After speaking with Louise, asking her to stay with Aggie, I headed for the station. Before leaving the hospital, I called the station. The Dumont woman and her confederate, Piaf, were being held in a cell away from the general population. I instructed the duty officer to place her in an interrogation room

226

under guard until I got there. No one was to talk to her.

"Which room?" I asked the duty officer when I managed to reach his desk through the usual press of people.

"Number two," he said, looking away from a heavyset woman in her forties who was demanding to speak to someone in charge. I had to bite my tongue to keep from telling her to shut up. "Sorry 'bout Pete. How's he doin'?"

"He'll make it."

I roughly pushed my way through a half dozen or so people toward the hall leading to the cell area and the interrogation room.

When I stepped into the windowless room, I saw Celeste Dumont sitting at the table. Her guard stood quietly against the wall behind her. I grabbed a chair and pulled it over to the table and sat down. She looked at me in silence. I could plainly see the contempt on her face and the anger burning hatred in her eyes.

"Save it," I said. "Now let's understand each other right from the start. I think you are a cold, calculating bitch that has been seducin' men to betray their country by providin' secrets to a Russian agent. What you're goin' to tell me is how many of these men have been workin' for him and their names."

"Go to hell," she spat.

"Yeah, well, we'll see who goes there first," I said. "I don't think you know the situation you're in, so I'll tell you. First, you are goin' to be charged as an accessory to murder in the deaths of at least two men. Then, you will be charged under the War Act for espionage as an agent of a foreign government. Both charges carry the death penalty. An' jus' so know, don't look for any breaks from me no matter how much you decide to cooperate. I plan to be at your execution an' watch you swing."

I suddenly heard myself. I have never felt or acted this way before in all my years as a cop. Then I realized just how angry I was feeling, thinking of Pete lying in the hospital and Aggie's anguish. I pushed the chair back and stood up, looking down at her.

"I can't look at you any longer. You make me sick. You best think real hard on what I've jus' told you."

I headed for the door.

"Put her back in the cell with the other one," I instructed the guard.

I left the room and went back to the duty officer's post and, standing behind him, told him I was leaving for Naval Headquarters.

I was sitting in our meeting room nursing a mug of coffee while I waited for Phil and Michael Parks. I was happy for the time to settle my nerves and anger despite thoughts from a few hours ago; images of those last minutes when Pete was shot and I killed the Russian.

The door opened and both men walked in and took their customary places at the table.

"You look like crap," Phil said. "What's up?"

It looked like they had not received word on the actions of a few hours ago.

"That's 'bout right," I said. "Bad news. The Russian's dead."

"What?" Michael said, raising his voice in surprise. "When and how?"

"A few hours ago, an' I shot him."

Phil and Michael exchanged quick glances then looked back at me; waiting.

I filled them in on what happened.

"Good lord," Michael said. "Is Pete...?"

"Outta surgery an' the doctor said he should recover."

"Thank God."

I went on with my account of the events leading up to the shootout.

"We found an address up on Edinburgh Street from those scraps of paper we took from the French woman's room which gave us a place to start lookin'. You know what I mean," I said to Phil, "I gave them to you, remember?"

"Yes, go on," he said.

"Anyway, it was Pete who figured it out with help from a contact he had at the phone company. Turns out they have a phone installed at that address to someone named Marcel Piaf. It struck us as too much a coincidence him bein' French an' the

Dumont woman, so I decided we would take a run up there an' check it out. Appeared my hunch was right." I paused for a moment then went on.

"Best I can figure out is someone inside the house must've made us because the next thin' I know they tried to make a break for it. Pete took off for the back of the house with me not far behind. I got there jus' as he got shot an' that's when the Russian saw me an' lined up on me. I got my shots off first."

"Where are the two accomplices?" Phil asked.

"At the station in a cell," I said.

"And what do you intend to do with them?"

"If I had my way she'd swing. I booked the woman as an accessory to murder an' attempted murder of a cop but the truth of the matter is I don't think the Crown will go for it. No direct evidence, so they'll probably walk."

"I may be able to do something," Michael said with a sly grin. "Maybe not to both of, but most definitely to the woman."

Phil and I looked at him.

"I believe that a case can be made against her because of her connection to the Russian in so far as she willingly enticed certain men to provide secret information to him."

"Good," I said, "that's bloody good. An' I think I'll make sure that Piaf decides to leave the city."

"Okay. That's settled then." He stood up. "As always Robie, thank you again for your excellent work and contributions; you and Pete. And do please convey my best wishes for a speedy recovery. Tell him I will try and stop by."

"Thanks, Michael, an' I will." We shook hands then he left Phil and I alone.

"That goes double from me," he said, shaking my hand.

"Me too," I said. "I'd say 'til next time but you know I'd be lyin'."

"I know."

We both chuckled as we headed for the door.

Epilogue

It was now three weeks since the Russian affair ended. Christmas was not far off and the kids were driving Louise and me crazy with questions about toys and gifts. Pete was home with Aggie and their little one. He was mending well but the experience of being shot had changed him. I understood that, remembering how I felt when I came back after the last war. Morrison made sure that he and his family were taken care of by the city, especially as Aggie left her job to stay home to nurse him back to health.

Shortly after Phil and Michael rounded up Larry Mitchell and Jack Markham, they were taken into custody by the RCMP and transported to Camp Debert, outside of Truro where they were held pending their trials for stealing military secrets and selling them to a Russian agent.

As for Nikolai Petrov, his body was sent to Ottawa and released to the Soviet Consul for disposition. I learned from Phil a week later that a formal protest was made to

Ottawa by the Consul claiming that the police exercised unnecessary and unlawful force when they killed an Allied Russian citizen. They were demanding action be taken against the police in Halifax. Lots of luck with that happening.

Celeste Dumont was charged as an accessory to murder. This was later dropped and she was charged with conspiring with a foreign agent to steal military secrets. She was transferred over to Naval Intelligence where, with Phil's intervention, had her released to the RCMP who wanted her for the information she had on the Separatist movement in Quebec. The last I heard, she ended up singing like a bird and was now serving a reduced sentence somewhere in La Belle Province.

Henry Wallace pleaded guilty to abetting a foreign agent and was sentenced to three years in Dorchester Prison in New Brunswick. His operation folded up almost overnight and his men scattered.

As for me? I am seriously thinking about calling it a day. The war took its toll on me, as it did to so many others. But it was more than that; everything seemed to be changing: the city, people, everything. It was feeling like I did not belong here anymore.

The city was alive with excitement. People were letting themselves believe the end was close. There was also something going on; a sense of impending doom. I felt it. The only difference was I sort of knew what it was and where it was coming from. For five long years, the roots of animosity between the population and the military festered just below the surface. I tried to alert Captain Morrison to the possibility of it blowing up, especially once the war ended. He agreed with me and presented his concerns to the mayor and city council, but politicians being politicians...

My thoughts were interrupted when my children came rushing in and swamped me in my chair to say goodnight. With a wide smile, I stood up and followed them upstairs to their room and, as was my custom, joined them in their nighttime prayers. I glanced at my wife, who stood in the door with her beautiful smile, and blew her a kiss.

The End

If you enjoyed this book, please leave a review.

Also published by BWL Publishing Inc.

The John Robichaud Mysteries
Dead Man In The Harbour
Murder On The Docks
The Evil Men Do
The Body In Room 103
The Norwegian Woman

Unfinished Business (A Novel)

Rum Bullets and Cod Fish – Nova Scotia
Canadian Historical Mysteries, Book 1

H. Paul Doucette has lived and worked in many countries throughout a varied career in International Transportation ranging from twelve years as a merchant seaman to a career as an industrial logistic specialist.

He spent a few years 'thumbing' his way across North America and Mexico during the cultural revolution of the sixties and early seventies, during which time he participated in the civil rights and antiwar movements of the time.

He has also enjoyed moderate success as a Fine Art Black and White Photographer. Now he is pursuing his interest as a writer of period set mysteries.

In addition to the Robichaud Mystery series he has also written two other series; one set in Greenwich Village in the 1960s and another war time series set in the Pacific.

He has been retired for more than twenty years and lives in Dartmouth, Nova Scotia.

BWL Publishing

bwlpublishing.ca

www.ingramcontent.com/pod-product-compliance
Lightning Source LLC
Chambersburg PA
CBHW070014120726
47909CB00003B/921